The Perks of being A Duchess

TANYA WILDE

A MIDDLETON NOVEL

This book is a work of fiction. Names, characters, businesses, organiza- tions, places, events and incidents either are the product of the author's imagination or are used fictitiously. Any resemblance to actual persons, living or dead, events, or locales is entirely coincidental.

THE PERKS OF BEING A DUCHESS Copyright © 2019 by Tanya Wilde. All rights reserved. Printed in the United States of America. No part of this book may be used or reproduced in any manner whatsoever without written permission except in the case of brief quotations em- bodied in critical articles or reviews. For information contact: Tanya Wilde at PO BOX 1403, George, Western Cape, South Africa 6530

Print Edition ISBN: 978-0-6398222-0-4
Didital Edition ASIN: 978-0-6398222-1-1

Cover by Marius Hoeksema

First Edition: 11/2019

For you, dear reader

For Marius.

By Tanya Wilde

Misadventures of the Heart

An Earl's Guide to Catch a Lady
A Lady's Guide to Kiss a Rake
A Gentleman's Guide to Save a Lady
Give Your Heart a Rake

The Middleton Sisters

An Invitation to Marriage
The Perks of Being a Duchess

Lords of Scandal

Swept Away by a Wild Lord
Swept Away by a Wicked Rogue

MacCallan Clan

A Gypsy in Scotland
The Highlander Who Loved Me

Ladies Who Dare
Not Quite A Rogue

Chapter 1

When a Middleton caused a scandal, it was never by half measures. In fact, they usually engaged in the exact amount of caution one would when casting one's fate entirely to the wind. And this was certainly the case with Willow Middleton, who had thrown every bit of care into the mid-May breeze.

Willow inhaled deeply, smoothing her hands over the soft pink silk wedding gown with a growing sense of resolve. It was often said new relationships held the promise of a bright future, a future with love, happiness and prosperity.

The Perks Of Being A Duchess

Whoever said that ought to be run through with a blade, Willow thought darkly as she and her father reached the edge of the aisle she was about to walk down. As far as promises go, she was not feeling any kind of promise—except the promise of infamy.

But there was one memory that came to mind in this moment.

Willow had once advised her sister, Poppy—quite teasingly—whenever the day should come where she lost her marbles, she ought to take care to wear her best gown for the occasion.

Willow had never thought a day would come when she'd be the one following her own advice. She smoothed her hands over her skirts. Well, nearly following it. This was not her best dress, after all—it wasn't even her dress to begin with.

"So much for that then," she muttered under her breath, dropping her gaze to regard the exposed flesh of her ankles. It wasn't as though she had planned, or even prepared, for this to be the day she descended into madness. It had come on rather suddenly, a wild impulse that had replaced all common sense.

And this was by far the craziest, most impetuous and reckless thing she'd ever done. Far bigger than the odd prank she'd played here and there. Colossal even, for it entailed handing over the oh-so-small thing called her life and pledging it to another.

The Duke of St. Ives.

The man her sister had deserted at the altar only moments ago.

Beside her, her father stood tall, proud. Her rock. Willow hoped he would still be that proud after today was through. But for better or worse, there was no turning back now.

"Are you ready, dear?" Her father's soothing voice tugged at her twelve-year-old self—a time where her only thought had been colorful ribbons and pretty bonnets.

As ready as I will ever be.

In answer, she took a resolute step toward her fate just as the wedding march struck up, each chord slamming into her chest with the subtlety of a nail driving into a piece of wood.

But there was peace in knowing she was saving her sister from ruin at least, particularly seeing as she had her own selfish reasons for wedding the duke.

That was the true secret—the reason for her impulsive actions. She could fool everyone—her family, St. Ives, and even the guests—that she wed the duke to save her sister. But she could not fool herself.

In her chest, a cauldron of emotions churned.

Willow knew that she had quite willingly descended into this madness. She was walking down the aisle because she wanted to, because her sister had provided her the perfect opportunity to do so.

Truth be told, she wasn't even sure her actions *would* save Holly's reputation. She may very well worsen everything with her efforts this day. But she took another step forward anyway.

Madness. Utter madness.

Willow clung to that madness like a lifeline. It was the only way she managed to put one foot before the other. So much was at stake.

But for every step she took, her heart stuttered to a stop and then charged into a full beat again. The duke could still discover her deception, even though she wore a veil thick enough to obscure her face.

She was, after all, a few inches taller than her sister—a fact made obvious by the length of the dress. For anyone looking closely, it would be a telltale clue that duplicity was underfoot. Willow prayed the duke only saw the shortened dress as a final rebellion on his fiancée's part.

In truth, his reaction upon finding a different bride under the veil was the real cause for concern. Would he be humiliated beyond belief? Would he annul the marriage?

Willow supposed the worst that could happen was that the duke marched off in a fury upon the discovery, leaving her and her fleshy ankles to the mercy of the wolves. But even as she considered that, she felt the combination of the duke's arrogance and male pride would demand he go through with the wedding regardless. At least, she hoped that would be the case.

Darting her eyes to the row on her left, then to her right, Willow became aware of curious eyes dropping to her slippers, whispers reaching her from all sides.

Willow's ears burned.

Fortunately, her father hadn't seemed to notice either of her fashion faux pas. Not only was the shortened skirt an issue, but it was also rather out of fashion to wear a veil. She also sensed her father's worry for her—or rather for Holly, the "her" he thought she was—since the wedding had been hastily patched together. They had all been worried, in fact, but Holly had insisted she had found her true love.

That proclamation had lasted all but four days.

Nevertheless, her father still believed Holly to be madly in love with St. Ives, which is why he was presently walking the bride down the aisle and not dragging her away from it.

Speaking of which, her bridal march was nearly over. Just six or so steps away, the intimidating figure of the duke loomed. She straightened her spine and prepared to face the man who would soon be her husband.

He stood impossibly tall, his face clear of all expression, hands clasped behind his back. He was as unbearably handsome as he'd always been with his sandy hair artfully arranged over his forehead, though that did not tame the natural wildness of his locks.

Willow understood why Holly had fallen hard and fast. Had it not been for his eyes—which ruined the perfection of his Adonis-like features in her opinion—she might have fawned over him as well.

She could not see them now, but if she closed her own, she could envision those soulless black pools, filled with nothing but fathomless indifference. A chill passed through her.

Think of your goal.
Think of your family. The scandal.
Remember he is a tyrant.

The last was a sobering thought, reminding her of the demands he would make of her, the demands which had caused her sister to fall right out of love with him.

But Willow could handle one duke. There would be a scandal all the same, but this way, at least, Poppy would have a fighting chance of finding a respectable husband. And Willow would get what she truly wanted—a child.

Grand adventures of falling in love? She'd leave that to her sisters.

But she did want a particular kind of love: the kind that lasted forever, the kind that only grew fiercer with time, and the kind that required a husband. So, when the opportunity to secure a husband without prancing before hordes of gentlemen, hoping they took notice, and then having to endure a lengthy courtship appeared, Willow had seized it.

Her desire for a child was finally within her grasp.

And she would be a duchess. There were worse things in the world.

"What on God's green earth are you doing?" An angry voice echoed through the church.

A hush fell over the ceremony like a heavy cloud and Willow was forced to a halt when her father stopped. Her knees almost gave out. Had she been caught out? Who did the voice belong to? Her heart skipped beat after beat, waiting.

But nothing.

Willow bit down on her lower lip and spared a nervous glance over her shoulder. When she found no enraged person, Willow let out a soft breath and nodded at her father, who led the last few steps to the duke.

St. Ives's expression, from what she could gather behind her veil, gave nothing away. Not even the slightest fire burned in his eyes. His features were vacant, as if he were bored with the entire ordeal. Did he not care that someone might have stopped the wedding? Or was he just *that* arrogant?

"Dearly beloved," the priest hastily began citing the words that would bind them together. "We are gathered together here in the sight of God…"

Doubt began to seep into her skin. She always thought her actions through. For the most part, Willow did not lunge and leap, consequences be damned. But now a nagging thought entered her mind. While she knew why she had acted impulsively, she knew nothing of why the duke wanted to be hastily wed.

It did not matter, she told herself. And it truly did not. Regardless of his reason, everyone won in the end, right?

Or so she hoped. Standing beside St. Ives, who was so tall and solid, it was hard not to feel the quiver of nerves that skittered up her spine, sending tiny bursts of sparks along her skin.

Willow was bursting with questions. Did he feel nervous too? Did he suspect she was not his chosen bride? Was he furious behind his mask of indifference?

Willow found herself further dwelling on why she ought to have waited to marry and perhaps not steal her sister's fiancé, abandoned though he may be. His anger, for one—he was a moody, broody lord. She could have married a quiet, endearing man instead. And, according to Holly, the duke had rules that must be followed. Strict rules. Rules that involved one slice of toast. Then there was her mother-in-law—the dragon duchess.

It almost seemed like she was marrying into a bad Shakespearean play.

Willow swallowed her misgivings. There was no turning back now in any case. Assuming they completed their vows, they were in this, for better and for worse.

"…have and to hold from this day forward…"

Think about tiny baby fingers and toes.

"…if either of you knows any impediment, why ye may not be lawfully joined together in Matrimony…"

Don't think about a bad Shakespearean play.

Willow half expected that same booming voice to call her on her deception.

No one spoke up.

"…have this woman to thy wedded wife, to live together after God's ordinance in the holy estate of Matrimony? Wilt thou love her, comfort her, honor, and keep her in sickness and in health; and, forsaking all others, keep thee only unto her, so long as ye both shall live?"

Willow held her breath.

Don't say no. Don't say no. Don't say no.

"I will." The firm, strong voice of St. Ives echoed.

The air whooshed from her lungs.

"Wilt thou have this man to thy wedded husband. . ." *Yes! Yes! Yes!* She repeated over and over until the priest finished, ". . . so long as ye both shall live?"

"I will," she rushed to say and was pretty certain her reply had come out as a croak.

"Who giveth this woman to be married to this man?"

Her father stepped forward and the priest passed her right hand over to the duke in ceremonious custom.

Willow felt her breath catch.

For such an iron-fisted man, his touch was surprisingly gentle. Her hand trembled in his as she stared up into inscrutable eyes while he repeated his vows. *I, Ambrose Jonathan Griffin, take thee* Miss *Middleton as my. . .*

Wait a minute! He hadn't used Holly's name. Why hadn't he used her name?

Willow had no time to ponder the question before it was her turn to repeat her vows. "I, *Miss*," — she was not about to announce her name loud and clear if he hadn't — "Middleton, take this man . . ." *sickness and health and so forth and so forth and not obey* "according to God's holy ordinance; and thereto I give thee my troth."

His hand applied subtle pressure on hers.

Well, Willow *had* deliberately left out the *obey* part. Again, she wondered why he hadn't announced her sister's name.

Then he slipped the ring onto her finger — the final symbol of the fate she'd chosen — and Willow felt the touch deep in her bones.

And she realized, *he knew.*

Why else would he announce his name but not hers? Why else would his movements be as stiff as a stick as he slipped the ring onto her finger?

The remainder of the ceremony passed in a daze. Then, too soon — much too soon — his hands reached out to lift the veil. She'd have preferred to pass through the entire ceremony without lifting the veil, to reveal her identity in the carriage. Or after the wedding feast. Or tomorrow. But the duke had other plans.

Because he knew.

He must know.

Tension tightened in her chest as he lifted the layers of lace from her face, and she could not help holding her breath.

The moment of reckoning had arrived.

Their eyes locked.

Time stopped.

All around them, whispers of confusion rocked the church. And for the first time since Willow was introduced to the duke, a kaleidoscope of emotion—affirmation, disbelief and fury—flashed in the depths of his dark gaze.

But besides the subtle clench of his jaw, his composure remained untouched to the average observer.

Oddly, Willow felt nothing but relief. The duke was not a demon spawn, the very devil himself, bereft of any feelings. Deep, deep, so very deep down, the man possessed a heart.

Another realization followed shortly after that. They had yet to sign the registry. And even then, the marriage could still be annulled. Lord almighty, there were a thousand holes in her plan. Large holes. Holes that could ruin her entire family. And he knew it.

Obsidian eyes stared down at her.

Heat rushed to her cheeks.

Don't you dare annul this marriage, her eyes challenged.

And then, before Willow knew what he was about, his head bent to capture her lips in a kiss. It was so unexpected, so shockingly brazen, that her hands lifted and pressed against his chest and pushed, eyes wide. Beneath her fingers, his muscles tightened, but he didn't move an inch, didn't draw his mouth away from hers.

It occurred to Willow then that his kiss was more than intentional. He meant for it to be a bold declaration. *This is my chosen bride*, the kiss seemed to imply. But merciful heaven, she felt that kiss right down to the tips of her toes, and of their own will, her lashes drifted shut. His lips were soft, such a contrast against his harder features. Her fingers gripped his jacket, anchored there, his teeth scraping her lower lip.

This was no mere peck.

The priest cleared his throat.

His lips pulled away, turbulent eyes lifting to hers. Then he leaned in, a sharp bite laced in his voice as he whispered, "Wife."

A promise of satisfaction.

Swiftly, the duke pivoted and signed his name across the registry. When he handed her the quill there was only the slightest hesitation before she did the same. He did not so much as glance at her signature, only held out his arm and waited for her to join him at his side.

Willow forced breath into her lungs. She had known what she was getting into, had known her actions would prompt some form of reaction from him. What she hadn't expected was the thrill of excitement that was now racing along the edges of her backbone.

Her fingers trembled as she placed them on the sleeve of his jacket. The raw strength of him rippled beneath her hand. Suddenly nervous, she listened to the quiet conversation and rustling of movement around her as her husband led her from the church. She didn't dare seek out Poppy or her father, not ready to face the confusion and shock of her family.

Again, she reminded herself that this was what she had wanted.

And it was. Except for one startling development.

Willow was taking notice of St. Ives in ways she hadn't before. Not once as her sister's betrothed had she noticed his scent or any detail about him except that he was tall, arrogant, detached, and a duke. Now, she pursed her lips together, inhaling the woody scent of her husband, drawing it deep into her lungs. It was a rich and earthy aroma, and quite pleasant. For a moment, Willow allowed herself to believe that perhaps this entire day would be as pleasant. After all, he hadn't stormed out of the church. He'd signed the registry. They were married.

If the worst possible thing had not happened, perhaps she'd pulled it off.

Willow nearly smiled.

Nearly.

Because what happened next was entirely without warning.

The loud wail of her mother-in-law filled the church.

Chapter 2

Ambrose Brandon Jonathan Griffin, the eighth—and arguably proudest—Duke of St. Ives, waited impatiently for his bride to stroll down the aisle. He had already reminded her once the ceremony would commence in four minutes time, and it was a mark of blatant rebellion to delay any longer than that.

He caught himself glancing at his pocket watch and slowly put it away. He knew it would be the only act that betrayed his impatience, because he knew no emotion betrayed his features. His mask was in place. Everything was in place. As it ought to be.

Everything except his bride.

Who was purposefully late, he was sure.

It was no secret, at least to him, that Holly Middleton did not wish to marry him. Not anymore. Not since she had glimpsed his true temperament.

Ambrose had watched firsthand as the stars faded from her eyes. The realization of what it would truly mean to be his wife had struck her then. He had borne witness to the girl's hopes and dreams vanish before his eyes. And any emotion welling up in his chest at the sight, like empathy, he had pressed down. Hard.

His heart had hardened a long time ago. There was nothing tender left inside of him to give. Emotion didn't sway him. Nothing held power over him. Even if he was so inclined to provide Holly Middleton a way out of their betrothal, he couldn't. His father's will had seen to that.

In the end, Miss Middleton had accepted her fate and the rules he had handed her. If her sudden reluctance had been noted by her family, none made any comment of it. Not that their disapproval would have made any difference. The betrothal agreement had been signed.

It was done.

He caught one of Holly's sisters surveying the church and had to suppress another wave of annoyance at his bride's lack of punctuality. That same displeasure had him seeking out his pocket watch again. To hell with what anyone thought.

What the deuce was taking her so long?

Finally—after what felt like eons—the bride appeared across the aisle and the piano started up. The tension in his shoulders eased.

She wore a veil. Not uncommon, though most brides preferred to do without them. This one wasn't particularly long, and it was layered. He could hardly make out any of her features. Did the veil hide swollen eyes from a night of weeping? Or a face flushed with misery?

But before he could ponder the matter further, Ambrose's attention was pulled to the rousing of hushed whispers. He surveyed the snickering guests with growing unease.

Inside his belly, his innards clenched.

His eyes darted back to Holly. She appeared the perfect bride. Her gown was fit for a duchess. Only . . . *What the bloody* . . . Creamy pale flesh met his view when his gaze lowered to the hem of her dress. Her skin stood out in stark contrast to the blue slippers that nestled on her feet.

Ambrose fought down the urge to scowl. What had Miss Middleton done?

This was all his fault. He should have known she'd act out in some way. The Middletons usually skirted around convention effortlessly enough. She had been bound to do something. He ought to have anticipated this. But call him mad, he hadn't expected Holly to make their wedding the spectacle of London.

Damn his father and the conditions of his will. He hadn't been able to find a single flaw in the document, and by Jove, he had searched. And because of that search, he had waited until the last possible moment to take a wife, leading him to partake in desperate measures to secure one. And now here he stood, waiting for the ankle-displaying Middleton chit to make her way down the aisle.

Had he a choice, Ambrose would not have taken a wife at all. Let the title pass to his brother, Jonathan and his offspring. It was the perfect solution. All tied up in a neat little bow.

Except his father hadn't agreed.

The man must be laughing in his grave this very minute.

And where was his brother anyway? He ought to have been here, beside Ambrose. Luckily no one had taken notice of his absence, compliments to his bride and her ankles.

What was Holly thinking? Did she mean to punish him? The rules were there for her well-being, to keep her healthy and strong. Was this one last attempt at defiance? Or the beginning of several?

Frustration rode him hard. Still, his mask never once slipped. Already, his brain devised a story to counteract any gossip. It would take much more than setting a new wedding trend to ruffle his proverbial feathers.

Then a booming voice called out, his words echoing off the walls of the church. At that, Ambrose admitted one little feather did ruffle. Fortunately, years of practice had awarded him with remarkable composure. He made sure that he did not move a muscle as silence stretched out like a vast ocean in response to the cry "What on God's green earth are you doing?"

Had the little minx arranged that too?

One could almost believe the voice belonged to God, seeing as, from his position at the front of the church, the voice had no shape or form attached to it.

What a spectacle.

When no further comment followed and no one appeared, he watched as his bride once again proceeded to make her way to him.

He let out a small breath.

Soon he would be married and all the unpleasantness of the past twelve months would be laid to rest.

Except he would be leg-shackled.

Nevertheless, Ambrose could move on with his life.

He paid enough attention to the ceremony to know when his lines were, but other than that, his mind wandered—mostly to his bride. His body prickled with awareness with her standing so close to him, her head stopping just shy of his shoulder. Her scent was different today. Not the fruity tone of orange blossoms he had come to expect from Holly, but more flowery.

Jasmine.

Soft. Light. Pure.

Ambrose gritted his teeth. What was he doing? He had no business noticing her scent. Neither did his body have any business seeking to inhale deep lungfuls of her air.

He was impatient for this matter to be settled, that was all.

One would think, in this day and age, they would have discovered a more convenient way to suitably marry other than submit oneself to this stretched-out pomp.

Why should a business arrangement be celebrated, in any case?

Ambrose hated public spectacles. If he had gotten his way, they'd be married privately with only a select number of witnesses. But his mother had insisted. *To keep up appearance*, she had said, because of the hasty nature of the marriage. And God help him if he did not give his mother what she wanted.

The one thing he hated more than public spectacles was a woman that wailed in his ears.

His mind drifted back to his bride. Had he not waited this long in search of an escape clause, had he just accepted his inevitable fate, he'd have taken his time in selecting a wife. A lady of demure stature. A wallflower, maybe. He would never have chosen Holly Middleton with her dreamy eyes and bleeding heart.

Ambrose could imagine those eyes, red and swollen beneath her veil. Except something about his betrothed gave him pause. It was hard to say why. The determined set of her shoulders? The blue slippers with her soft pink dress? Or perhaps it was the entire package. Something about her did not ring true. And suddenly and inexplicably, he was certain puffy eyes were not what he'd find.

His gaze flicked over her. Dread and something unnamable spread through him.

This wasn't Holly Middleton. This wasn't his bride.

The blue slippers did not provide for much height and Holly's head had never quite reached his shoulder. Now, it suddenly did.

He peered down at the woman, studying her with the unwavering attention of a predator. It was *a* Middleton, but not the one he had agreed upon to marry.

His eyes darted to where her sister sat in the front row. He couldn't recall the chit's name. Something flowery. And there was a sister missing. He couldn't recall her name either, except for the frosty looks she'd always cast him whenever he called upon Holly. The chits had always just been Miss Middleton to him.

Ambrose marveled at the lack of attention he had paid. Usually he was much more astute when it came to names. But he hadn't bothered to take much note of his bride's sisters—or their names. There had been matters of more importance to occupy his mind and they, well, they were just *there*.

A duty. An annoyance. A necessity.

Ambrose almost dragged a hand over his face then and there. He was tired. It had been a long year. Perhaps he was imagining things. This could simply not be happening to him.

Behind him, scores of eyes burned into his back. Ambrose knew that weddings were nothing but theatre where one entertained an audience with all the props of the latest fashions, but he couldn't shake the feeling that his bride was going to give them much more than what they came for—that she'd give them a real show.

When the ceremony finally came to the portion where they repeated their vows, he tensed, but his voice was firm and resolute as he repeated his vows. Then his eyes drifted over her concealed face as she repeated her own.

"I, Miss Middleton—" his hands twitched, "—take this man to be my wedded husband . . ." The voice confirmed it. This wasn't Holly Middleton. ". . . Death us do part, according to God's holy ordinance; and thereto I give thee my troth."

Another proverbial feather rose.

Whoever this woman was, she had left out an important part of her vows. Which brought him to the question: what the hell was he going to do? He had precious little options—no options, in fact—but to see this through, thanks so his father's will.

All the same, that did not stop him from spending the remainder of the ceremony pondering, arguing and debating the best course of action.

And after, when it became apparent his wife would never lift the damn lace from her face, he reached out and lifted the thing, already knowing, but still praying, he was wrong.

He wasn't.

Sky-blue eyes stared up at him, set in a face that didn't belong to his betrothed. Astonishment engulfed him even though deep down he'd known. The emotion was so unexpected he had no time to school his features from the shock.

His mask slipped.

For one, gut-wrenching moment, Ambrose felt exposed, as though she, *this* Miss Middleton, could see straight through his purposely erected armor.

Fury began to unfold in the inner reaches of his heart.

Ambrose had been deceived.

Outwitted.

Jilted.

He dropped a curtain over any emotion, pushed down his disbelief. In its place rage churned, retaliation beckoned.

A tiny part of him, a sliver of thought really, wondered whether it mattered. He was married. His father's will was met. Perhaps he should leave it be. But that was only a fleeting moment of weakness. It bloody well did matter. It was a matter of principle. And pride. He was a Duke. Powerful. And he had been tricked. He had been weighed and found wanting by Holly bloody Middleton. On the day of their wedding.

He would not stand for it!

Ambrose noted with some measure of satisfaction that a flush crept across his bride's cheeks as she recognized his anger.

This Middleton possessed some sense.

Ambrose ignored the rising chatter of the guests. Out of the corner of his eye, he could see some of their heads bent low, attempting to piece together whether they had gotten the details of the wedding wrong. But Ambrose knew what the invitation read. He had written the lines himself. This would turn into a nightmare if he did not put a stop to it right this moment.

So he did the only thing that came to mind.

He lowered his head and kissed the bride.

At first, he felt her hand rest against his chest and half-heartedly push, but he did not stir. Before the entire Church, before their family, before God, he claimed her as his. She and her sister might have tricked him, but over his dead body would he allow the *ton* to question their union. The kiss made his position clear—she was his chosen bride.

Then she breathed a soft note of peppermint into him and Ambrose found himself knocked off balance. The delicate curve of her lips softened beneath his and the sensation hit him like a ton of bricks.

He felt her grip his lapel in response to his tongue grazing along her lower lips. She was holding onto him, pulling him closer. But even her sultry, pliant mouth wasn't truly what caused his heart to hammer in his chest. It was the sweet flavor of the fragrance mixed on her skin, the light notes of jasmine that elevated him to heaven.

A throat clearing broke the spell and Ambrose pulled away from her. Bewilderment swamped him. He glared down into equally dazed cerulean eyes with grim displeasure.

So the kiss had stirred her too? Well, he would pretend his lips didn't burn at the loss of contact. But he did intend to warn her that there would be no backing away from this commitment, no running like her sister, so he leaned forward and whispered *wife* in her ear.

The word sent a zap of something sharp through him. He pushed the unruly feeling aside. What he needed to do was gather his wits to salvage the situation, not feel unfamiliar sensations.

Ambrose turned away and swiftly signed the registry and waited for his wife to do the same.

Done. It was done.

He offered his arm, keeping his features cool, not daring to betray how much she or that kiss had disturbed him. He strolled past all the curious stares, back straight and head held high like he wasn't a duke that had just been duped.

Wouldn't that make for a grand title in the gossip rags?

In truth, Ambrose was on the verge of exploding. Only those who knew him well would recognize his rigid posture for what it was: fury. And he was furious.

But these people, this flock of vultures, would see nothing but an arrogant duke.

Ambrose cringed at the familiar wail of his mother.

Not bloody now.

Where the hell was his brother when he needed him most? Now Ambrose had to deal with a treacherous little wife and a caterwauling mother on his own.

The dowager's reaction would only fuel the gossip. She ought to know that weeping at such a time would cause rumors to rampage. Especially now when it was crucial to keep up appearances.

Ambrose shook his head, his mind spinning. He would deposit his wife in the waiting carriage and then he'd return for his mother.

But first.

"What is the meaning of this?" he hissed between clenched teeth in his wife's ear.

"The meaning of what?" His bride countered, smiling at one of the guests.

"You know very well what I'm referring to."

"Then you ought to have no trouble understanding the meaning of what just happened."

"I understand a great deal. What I want to know is why I find myself married to you and not your sister."

"I daresay you know the answer to that question as well."

Was that censure he detected in her tone? From *her*?

Ambrose wanted to shake her. Growl. Kick something. Hard. Never in his life had he felt this rattled before. Not even when he had read the conditions of his father's last words. Was this what marriage would always be like? Constantly angry? Forever swindled by one's wife?

Once outside, he stiffly ushered her into their waiting carriage. He could hear his mother just behind them, and already his brain wove a tale of mothers and emotions and weddings. She was prone to dramatic behavior, after all. Everyone in London was aware of that.

A good number of guests had followed them out, along with the still-wailing dowager. He could hear them openly speculating about the bride. Somewhere off to the right, Ambrose heard the words *heathen wedding swap,* and he shot a glare that way. The guests shrunk back at his withering look, and he turned back to the carriage just as his bride cast his mother A Look.

The woman was brazen, all right. Whether that was a good or a bad thing would yet be determined. But she had spunk; it bled from her like water seeping through small cracks littered over a wall.

Of their own volition, Ambrose's eyes dropped to her lips. His own began to tingle as he recalled their kiss. He wondered what his wife would make of it if she knew she'd been the first woman he had ever kissed in such a sensual manner. That he had only been with one woman his entire life—his former mistress—and they never kissed. At least not beyond the occasional peck on the temple or cheek.

That had been her one rule.

She had claimed kissing was an act more intimate than intercourse, and their arrangement was one for pleasure and not intimacy. Ambrose had left it at that. But that was then, and this was now.

Just then, his mother's wailing suddenly stopped.

Ambrose frowned and swung around. Had his mother suddenly controlled herself? He doubted it.

What the bloody . . .

Surrounded by a circle of London's worst gossips, his mother—in a heap of crumpled taffeta silk—lay sprawled in the dirt.

Hell.

Chapter 3

The mark of a great man, some would say, is his ability to navigate through impossible situations with great ease. Willow's husband appeared to be such a man. Other than his initial slip in countenance, one that had pleased her more than she cared to admit, not once did he betray emotion, even though he must be furious. It was simply impossible to tell from looking at him. But he had *known*. Somewhere during the ceremony, something had alerted him to her deceit.

And still he married her.

Bittersweet emotion centered in her chest.

She was wed to the stick-in-the-mud Duke of St. Ives. But she was married. She had done it. She had pulled it off by the skin of her teeth, but she had done it. Whether she would remain wed, Willow supposed, was another matter. Annulment was still an option.

Of course, that would leave her entire family in ruin. The papers would have a blast with this scandal as it was. Willow could just imagine the title should the duke annul the marriage. *The Great Deception: Miss Middleton jilts The Duke of St. Ives only for the duke to jilt Miss Middleton.*

Willow settled into the carriage just in time for the arrival of her sobbing mother-in-law. She shot the dowager a disapproving look.

The woman was making everything worse with her tears.

And then, to Willow's amazement, the dowager collapsed into a pile of heaping skirts.

The scene was truly remarkable.

The duke swore and rushed to his mother's side. Two footmen hurried to assist while another woman, with a hat that resembled a furry creature, revived the dowager with smelling salts.

Willow let out a sigh. The day had only just begun and she was ready for it to end.

Seconds later, her mother-in-law was settled in the carriage next to her son, who installed himself across from Willow.

A crowd had gathered, tittering behind their fans, rudely speculating about the turn of events. Just before the carriage door shut, Willow glimpsed Poppy, her face pale as a sheet of paper, eyes round with shock.

I'm sorry, Willow mouthed before Poppy was replaced by the drawn velvet curtains of the carriage door. Remorse clawed at her heart. The sisters told each other everything. And today they stood divided. Holly did not know what Willow had done and she, in return, did not know where her sister had run off to. Poor Poppy, she knew even less than the both of them.

The entire morning had been a hellish whirlwind. At least the duke had not been deserted at the altar. That ought to count for something. But one glance at his hard features told Willow it would not be as simple as all that.

"How could this have happened?" The Dowager cried. "Oh, the horror!"

Willow studied the woman in silence, peering at her from beneath her lashes. Mostly to avoid the scrutiny of St Ives. Years of pampered lifestyle had done nothing to halt the fine lines of the woman's timeworn skin. Her salt and pepper hair should have afforded her a more seasoned appearance. Instead, her milky, fatigued eyes suggested a more dismal spirit.

"We must dissolve this travesty immediately!" The dowager carried on.

Willow gave her a sharp look. She did not want the dowager to influence the duke's mind about dissolving their marriage. Holly had mentioned the Dragon

Duchess had commandeered the wedding arrangements, hence the name. Would the woman attempt to commandeer the outcome of this marriage, too?

Willow risked a glance at her husband, startled to find those black eyes scrutinizing her, noting every little nuance of her reaction, she was sure.

She held his gaze, refusing to be intimidated. If Willow were to remain his wife, he ought to be aware she did not cower under frosty glares, and refused to be bullied by anyone, even a man as powerful as he.

"The marriage will not be dissolved." His eyes never left hers. His voice brooked no argument.

Willow was not about to argue.

"Oh! The shame!" The dowager sobbed.

It was enough to provoke a flash of annoyance.

Apparently, the duke thought so too for he sent his mother a look of displeasure to which the duchess sniffed and looked away—silenced.

"Where is your sister?" St. Ives asked, turning his attention back to Willow.

"I've no idea," Willow said, shivering when those black eyes fixed on her. For the first time, she wondered how she was going manage a husband if he proved completely unmanageable. Up until now, she had stood firm in her mind that she could. She already knew he was imperious, but what if he was unbendable?

What if he would not give an inch?

And she needed him to give at least two inches—to gain his trust and to save her sister from the brunt of his anger. Beyond that, it did not quite matter, she supposed. She wanted a child. He required an heir. The math was simple.

"I find that hard to believe," the duke was saying. "She was present when last I reported the time. So, I imagine, were you."

"Holly is unaware that I took her place," Willow admitted. "I was supposed to draft a note for my father to find and leave."

The duke said nothing, just stared at her.

God help her, her gaze dropped to his lips for the briefest moment before shooting back to his eyes again. A knowing glint flashed in their depths. They were in a battle of wills, she realized. And she had lost this round.

Willow sat up straighter. She could not lose composure again underneath his gaze. Even if it pained her. Which it did. Ramrod stiff had never been her chosen position and at that moment, with the wailing Dragon Duchess on one side and a temperamental husband across from her, Willow wondered whether this would be the premise of their relationship. Her life.

Chaos.

"So instead of penning a note, you married me instead? To save your family from scandal, I presume?"

"Something like that," Willow murmured.

"On my life, this family is going down in infamy!" The dowager responded with a sulk.

It took an infinite amount of willpower to not roll her eyes. If anyone was going down in infamy, it would be Willow.

"So your sister does not know you took her place and you don't know where she ran off to," St. Ives clarified. "Is that correct?"

Willow lifted a haughty chin. "Yes. But even if I did know, I would not tell you."

"Such loyalty," he murmured. "One way or another, *wife*, I will find her."

Willow inhaled a low, deep breath. Her husband was a striking man. One might easily forget just how bossy he was by staring at the man.

"I am in possession of a name, you know."

He jerked, the movement subtle, but Willow noticed the slight jolt. "You do know my name, do you not?" she remarked dryly.

A sudden air of stillness surrounded him, and Willow saw the exact moment he concluded that he, in fact, did not.

"You cannot recall my name, can you, *Ambrose*?" she echoed incredulous. "I am in complete shock."

"Of course I know your name," he snapped, and smirked. "Willa."

"That is a nice name, Willa, but it's not mine."

His brows drew together in a fierce scowl, and this time Willow suppressed a smile. If he wished to learn her name, he'd have to ask. Or hope for someone to call her by her name. Because a man like him would never ask.

"Winnifred."

Unbelievable.

"I'm not acquainted with anyone by that name."

The dowager moaned. "Oh, how will I ever set foot in society again?"

They both ignored her.

"Wendy."

"Really, *Ambrose*, you should stop."

"It has something to do with a tree," he muttered.

Honestly.

"It also rhymes with pillow."

His features contorted into a dark scowl. "Damnation, tell me, then," he growled.

"Why do you wish to know the whereabouts of my sister?" Willow countered. She suspected she wasn't going to like the answer. Holly had to be protected at all cost.

"Your sister made a spectacle of me," St. Ives answered.

"You weren't jilted," Willow pointed out.

"Do you imagine just because you stepped in, your sister will be released from the consequences of her actions?"

"Yes?" Willow drew out the word.

"Have you any thought on how it feels to be so publically made a fool?"

Willow's heart dropped to her stomach. No, she did not. But all the same, beyond her own reasons for marrying the duke, she must protect her sister.

"I took her place, is that not enough?" she implored.

"That won't absolve her from the consequences, no."

His dismissive tone sparked her temper. "And what consequences are those?"

He shrugged. "She will marry my brother, Jonathan."

She jerked forward in her seat. *What?*

The man had just discovered the deception! How had he already plotted a plan of reckoning?

"And how long did it take for you to decide that?" Willow demanded.

"About as long as my astonishment lasted when I discovered I had been betrayed by my betrothed."

Willow snapped her brows together. His astonishment, as he called it, had lasted only a blink of an eye. "That seems harsh, does it not? Can we not come to another sort of understanding?"

"It seems perfectly appropriate that she marry my brother as I have wed her sister, do you not agree?"

"An eye for an eye, you mean."

"If that's how you wish to see it."

"Your logic is archaic," Willow rejoined.

"Maybe," the duke returned. "But if saving your sister from the consequences of her actions was why you happily took her place, you have grossly underestimated your position."

"Well," Willow said with a petulant pout, "I would not go so far as to say happily. But I had thought you would spare my sister your anger. Plus, I *am* the oldest sister. By rights, I ought to have been married first. And before you attempt to bully me, you should know that I will always protect my sisters. Nothing and no one can force me to do otherwise, including you."

"Commendable."

Willow quelled a shiver at the deep timbre of his voice. Lud, she had to be careful. He might be her husband, but in this matter, he was her adversary. "So what happens now?"

"We attend the wedding breakfast." His eyes turned frosty. "You will sit, smile prettily, and not mention a word of what transpired today. For all intents and purposes, it was you I courted. As far as anyone is concerned, you were always meant to become my wife."

You were always meant to become my wife.

In another life, with another man, those words would have melted her insides. From him, only coldness settled in her belly.

"As you wish. But why punish my sister? Won't that raise unnecessary questions?" Willow attempted to call on his logic.

"It's a matter of principle."

"You mean pride."

"Call it what you wish, the outcome remains the same."

Oh, it will not, Willow vowed. One way or another, she would change his mind. "Perhaps you can tell me why you wanted to marry in haste in the first place?"

"Perhaps you can tell me the whereabouts of your sister," he countered.

Willow sighed. The man was determined to be difficult. Not that she could blame him; his pride had taken a blow.

"And just so we are clear, *wife*," he said with an infuriating amount of authority, "I am not a man swayed by the tears of a woman, if you were thinking of using them on me."

"No, I suppose you are not," she said, sparing a glance at her sniffing mother-in-law. No indeed, he was not. The poor woman had swooned and the only emotion it had elicited from her son was annoyance. Credit, it was annoying, but nonetheless.

Willow studied her husband from beneath the rim of her lashes. Somewhere inside him, an honorable man resided, she was certain of it. Even if it was dim hope, she was determined to find and appeal to *that* man.

Once again, she found her gaze dropping to his lips and then jerked them down to her hands. She had developed an unhealthy obsession with her husband's mouth. It was that kiss. Merciful heaven, it had overpowered all of her senses.

She wondered if the dowager would swoon again if the duke kissed her now, right here. Or how would they both react if she kissed him? Willow pushed the tempting image from her mind. There was still a wedding breakfast and her family's questions to get through. Not to mention, saving her sister from the duke's plot.

Settling deeper into her seat, she shut her eyes, closing the curtain on his penetrating gaze. If he expected her to wilt under his scrutiny, to bow her head and capitulate, to lay down her arms . . .

She would not give an inch if he did not.

Chapter 4

The wedding breakfast of blazing stares. That had been the total sum of Willow's thoughts at the wretched affair — and it was thankfully over. It had been quite unnerving to behold. She had never seen so many withering glares across one table. A cold, tiring affair, indeed. But then, that wasn't surprising given this day had not meant to be hers.

Nonetheless, her beloved cousins, Bradford and Quinn, had taken turns sending her new husband dark, threatening looks. Her father, bless his soul, had shot them warning glances. This, Willow suspected, was to insist on keeping the matter civil—the matter no one had spoken a word about.

But it hadn't ended there. Poppy had peered with narrowed eyes at the Dragon Duchess whenever the dowager sniffed and groused on about dignity and length of wedding dresses. And between her woeful bemoaning, her mother-in-law made sure to cast Willow dirty looks. As if she alone was responsible for all the wrongdoing in the entire world.

Willow, for the most part, only glowered at Poppy, who purposefully goaded her mother-in-law with snappish remarks about said wedding dress.

St. Ives, for his part, had glared at everyone. Or at least Willow thought he had. In his heart. One couldn't rightly tell by looking at him, mask and all.

It was fortunate, Willow mused, that no guests had been invited to the breakfast. A detail she had learned the duke had insisted upon. The unspoken truce would never have lasted under the pressure of the shrewd eyes of the *ton*. And even then, there were servants to be concerned with as far as gossip went—ergo, their silent agreement to not mention Holly's name. And, Willow thought too that perhaps everyone had tacitly agreed to a small period for emotions to cool, whatever good that had done them.

And Willow supposed no one had wished to incur the wrath of St. Ives since he had every right to be furious. It was inevitable, of course. Everyone had waited for him to explode—which to his credit and everyone's relief, he had not.

While frosty glares had been the main dish of the day, Willow still held hope that not much lasting damage had been done. Holly was tucked away somewhere safe for the moment and, with time, her husband would come to see reason.

God willing.

So with nothing to be done but wait or join in on the glaring contest, Willow's thoughts had turned to her impending wedding night. And then promptly turned away.

Towards the champagne.

Glass after glass.

Of course, St. Ives's hawk eyes hadn't missed this, and his lips pursed tighter with each sip she took. She noted that small sign of displeasure because, like a moth drawn to a flame, her eyes were drawn to those full sultry lips. And every time she looked at them, she took another sip. It apparently mattered little whether she liked him or not; every time those eyes fell on her, they set her blood on fire.

Then, as if being obsessed with his lips wasn't enough, she found herself wondering if their consummation would be as hard and unyielding as the man, or if there was another side to him, a more sensual side.

Cue more champagne. But no matter how much she sipped and sipped, her thoughts stayed with her.

Indeed, they had accompanied her straight through the breakfast and into her new bedchamber—her present whereabouts—feet planted firmly in the center of the room.

She cast an uncertain glance at the bed, then at the door adjoining their chambers. Would her husband expect her to wait in his chamber? Like, say, reclining on his bed? Naked?

Would *he* be naked?

Willow was no prude. A child had to be produced in some fashion. But the rest, the little intimate details of the deed, well, that remained a mystery.

She started at the sudden creak of the door. Expecting her husband, she whirled.

Poppy slipped into her room, shutting the door after her. "There you are! I have been looking everywhere for you!"

"Poppy!" Willow rushed over to her sister. "What are you still doing here? I thought everyone had left."

"They did, well, all except for father and Bradford. They are in the study with your husband, so I decided to loiter around and eavesdrop."

"Of course you did," Willow murmured, bemused.

"Not to mention one of my sisters ran off on her wedding day, and the other took her place," Poppy said, and then made a generous motion toward her face. "And, might I add, all without informing me to ready my jaw movements for the big reveal. Are you all right? I didn't want to leave before speaking with you."

Willow collapsed on the edge of the bed. "I'm terribly sorry, Poppy."

"There is no need to apologize, dear. Just tell me what happened. How did all this come about?"

Willow took a deep breath. "When I went to go check on Holly one last time, I found her quite put out, Poppy. She was in a complete state of panic. Not only did she not wish to marry St. Ives, but she said that he'd deceived her horribly." She paused, glancing at her sister. "I told her to go and I . . ."

"Decided to take her place?" Poppy said, giving her an appraising look.

"Yes."

"That does not make any sense. Why would you take her place if he is such a beastly man? Father would've made sure she'd gotten out of the marriage if that's what she wanted."

"Yes, Father would have. But then, what about you? Or me? Or even Holly someday? All our prospects—our family name—would've been completely ruined. And jilting a duke at the *altar*...not even we can skirt convention that much, Poppy."

Poppy sat down on the bed beside her with a huff. "You're right, Willow. But to marry him? What about the deceit he pulled on Holly?"

"That he's truly more of a beast than a knight in shining armor, you mean? Anyone but Holly could see that. Granted, the man is as austere as they come—and something about rules, Holly said. But I can handle one man. I didn't promise to obey him, after all."

Poppy smirked at that. "I suppose Holly would have run off eventually, but at least this way she might still find the love she is so eagerly in search of."

"Or she'll stumble into more trouble," Willow muttered. "Let us hope for the former."

"Oh, I wager she will have the time of her life," Poppy said, blue eyes sparkling. "But what about you, Willow? Now that you are married to the man Holly ran away from?"

With a groan, Willow rose and swept to the window. "Honestly? I have a feeling that he might not be as beastly as all that. I know it's bizarre to say, given how little I know him, but I just have a feeling. At any rate, I won't be having the time of my life just yet." Willow turned to her sister. "Is that odd?"

"Everything about this is odd," Poppy said, falling back against the pillows. "I spoke to Holly, you know. She was as shocked as I by the turn of events."

"You spoke with her?" Willow said in a hushed voice, glancing at the adjoining door.

Poppy sat back up. "It's safe to talk. Father's with the duke, remember?"

"Right, I suppose the contracts must be amended now," Willow murmured. "As well as the marriage license."

"At least you are a duchess, which ought to be some comfort."

"That is beside the point."

"It is?" Poppy said with a sly wink. "I reckon the perks will keep you happy, if not your husband's stellar body."

"Poppy!"

"The man watched you like a hawk at breakfast, you know. I thought he was afraid you might jump up and run, too."

"I wouldn't get very far," Willow muttered, trying hard not to think about any perks involving her husband. In any case, she had the sense St. Ives would physically shackle her to him if it prevented her from leaving. He had said an annulment wasn't an option. Whether for pride or his reason for a rushed marriage, he wanted to remain married as much as she did.

"You may be right. I cannot imagine a man like that giving up anything of his."

Anything of his.

Willow knew she wasn't supposed to feel a thrill at the word "his" but damn if it didn't rouse the pressure in her blood. It pained her, this sudden attraction to the duke. A day ago, he had been Holly's betrothed. It seemed laughable to indulge in fancies about him now when just hours ago any thoughts on him had been dismissive.

"I'm worried about you, Willow," Poppy murmured softly, crossing over to join her at the window. "I do not wish for you or Holly to be unhappy. It feels like I have lost two sisters this day."

"You have not lost us, dear," Willow murmured. "And this was my choice. I could not let Holly marry a man she did not love, not when she had been so hopeful about the subject. And while I did not plan for this to happen, when I was standing there, something came over me, and here we are."

"Yes, and while I appreciate the sacrifice, I would be remiss if I failed to point out that it's not too late to run. The marriage has not been consummated, and Father will call for an annulment if you ask him."

"You just said the duke would not give up what he considers his."

"Yes, I did. But on this point, the law outweighs his pride. You are my sister, and I want you to be happy."

"I cannot run now, Poppy, I've spoken *vows*."

"So *un*speak them."

Willow shook her head, giving Poppy an exasperated look. Her sister, who much resembled her cousin Belle, the Countess of Westfield, for her adventurous spirit, meant well, but she was not being sensible. An annulment would be as bad as a jilting. But, in truth, Poppy also wasn't aware of the desire that had driven Willow into action—and that was Willow's fault. It was time she put that to rights.

"I must tell you the whole truth, Poppy. Saving our family from scandal is not the only reason I married the duke. I didn't just do it for Holly, or you, or our family, I did it for myself, as well."

"What do you mean?" Poppy glanced at her in confusion. "Oh, you mean because of your potential ruination—"

"No. I mean for me. Because I want a child."

"You want a *child*?"

"Yes, ever since I can remember," Willow admitted. "I thought that if I took Holly's place I could save our reputations and meet my own wish."

Poppy shut her mouth. "I . . . I didn't know. You never told us."

"It wasn't significant," Willow murmured. "Not at the time."

"Not significant? You commandeered Holly's wedding. I'd say it's colossal."

"When you put it like that . . ." Willow sighed. "I had difficulty in sharing in it. We always talked of adventures and fun, not of marriage and children. So when I saw an opportunity, I took it. I don't feel guilty for that."

Poppy lifted her hands in defense. "I am not judging you, Willow. But do you truly believe a child is the answer? Would you not wish to wait for the *right* man to bear a child with?"

"And who is the right man?" Willow asked in a dry manner. "A man that promises to move mountains for me?"

"Of course not," Poppy said with a small laugh. "Mountains cannot be moved, but imagine a man who understood you, the real you. That is something to hold out for."

"It is a lovely sentiment, Poppy," Willow murmured, placing her hand on her sister's. "But I have made my choice."

"All right then, if you are certain, I shall have your back," Poppy said thoughtfully, and after a moment added, "You know, I should have suspected something amiss when our sister did not endlessly wax poetic drivel about the duke anymore."

"We did warn her," Willow said, sliding a stray curl behind her ear. "She has always been prone to fall in love at the drop of a hat. But none of that matters anymore. Our family will be spared from scandal and your chances of making a good match will remain intact."

"Do not worry about my prospects." Poppy made a wry face. "The man I choose will be stronger than whatever battering my reputability has undergone."

"You say that now but what if all of society snubbed our entire family?"

Poppy shrugged. "It will blow over in time when some other scandal explodes and distracts everyone. You know how the people of London thrive on scandal. If anything, we will be invited to all the parties because of the blemish attached to our name."

"That's true," Willow said with a grin before she sobered. "The important thing is to shield Holly from the duke and his wrath. He is demanding she marry his brother, Lord Jonathan."

"Horrors, no!" Poppy exclaimed, a look of shock on her face.

"Indeed, I shall try and change his mind, but I'll need time. Speaking of which, you've stalled my questions long enough. You spoke to Holly? Tell me! Is she all right?"

"Well, Holly, you will never believe, is with the Marquis of Warton."

"Warton?" Willow asked, shocked. "That surly man? However did that come about?"

"Apparently he has agreed to whisk her off to the country. Though I overheard one of the servants say that the duke has dispatched men in search of Holly, even the roads to Derbyshire."

"Have you been eavesdropping the entire morning?" Willow asked, some of the tightness in her chest eased. Warton might be surly, but he was an honorable man and a friend of her cousin Belle's.

"What can I say? It is a skill."

"Just the same, of all the outcomes I considered, this one never crossed my mind—Holly running straight from her wedding into Warton's protection. Now that's a craft. I thought she'd seek refuge with our cousins."

A smile twisted Poppy's lips. "Our sister has found another champion—she must give me tips when this is all over."

"At least she will be safe, as safe as she can be with the duke after her. Let us hope she does not fall in love with Warton, as well. Just think about the drama."

"Do not even jest!" Poppy tossed a pillow at her. "She wishes to see you before you leave, Willow. She's worried about you. Warton shall send a carriage in case you can slip away."

"I shall try my best," Willow said, meeting Poppy's gaze. She wanted desperately to meet with Holly and feared her sister might feel some resentment toward her—that she would not understand what had driven Willow to do the very thing she'd run from.

"Good," Poppy leaned forward, glancing at the door. "But be careful. I overheard St. Ives order the servants to inform him of your whereabouts at all times."

Willow's eyes widened. "And you are only telling me this now?"

"I've had other things on my mind, you know."

"I cannot believe I have become a prisoner in my own home."

"It sounds rather thrilling to me." Poppy gave her a devilish smile.

"Of course it would. You are just as bad as Holly!"

Poppy shrugged. "Since you are quite decided on the matter, why not have a bit of fun with it?"

Willow sent her a bemused look. "Do you know the duke does not even know my name?"

"*No*," Poppy drew out, this time real shock on her face. "Are you serious?"

"Yes! And when he attempted to guess, he guessed wrong."

"How shocking! A husband that doesn't know his wife's name." Poppy's eyes glazed with unspent laughter. "I wonder if he recalls mine."

"I very much doubt it. But slow-witted or not, his guard is up. He may suspect I might sneak out."

"Then you must wait until the duke falls asleep," Poppy suggested.

"And what if he falls asleep next to me?" Willow said in a low voice. Now *that* seemed a thrilling prospect and she turned away before her sister could see her blush.

"I suppose crawling over him won't help?"

Willow spun around. "Do not say such things!" Because then she'd imagine them. In fact, she already was. The vision of the duke naked and her crawling over his powerful chest was slowly burning into her mind. Her face flamed.

"You are probably right. He would wake to you wriggling all over him."

Crawl. Wriggle. The idea of simply touching her husband, no matter what way, caused her heart to accelerate at a rapid pace.

This was a severe complication.

"No matter, I shall come up with a plan," Willow said resolutely. She *would* meet her sister tonight. "So, you do not believe me impossibly selfish for my decision?"

"Of course not," Poppy said. "There is no shame in seizing an opportunity when it presents itself. *Carpe diem*, correct? And you saved our family from ruin."

"I believe the correct phrasing is *carpe diem, quam minimum credula postero*."

"I never can remember the last part," Poppy said with a grimace. "It burns my ears just to hear it."

"Yes, well, it's not about just seizing the day because tomorrow may never come; it's about trusting in the future." Willow needed to believe that more than ever.

"If memory serves," Poppy corrected, "The last part means something along the lines of trusting as little as possible in the future."

Not where Willow was going with that . . .

"Whatever shall I do now that you are married and Holly has gone into retreat?" Poppy continued. "And probably having the time of her life."

"I am sure you will find a pot of trouble to stir," Willow said with wry amusement.

"If only that were true," Poppy said, eyes sparkling.

It was certainly true in Willow's case. She had stirred a great big pot. She didn't know where to start to become the wife she wished to be. Because from the second she had dressed in her sister's wedding gown, one thought had frozen her mind. A question, really, that had lodged itself right in the center of her heart.

Was this the beginning of a grand life, or the end of one?

Chapter 5

Boundaries. Rules. Limitations.

Ambrose thrived on them.

Required them.

A lack of them was what had gotten Celia, his sister, killed ten years ago. And Ambrose would never forgive himself for that. He ought to have taken better care of her. He ought to have done a great many things. But he could not change any of that now. He could, however, ensure that it never happened again.

Because Ambrose refused to suffer from the pain of such a loss again.

Ergo, rules.

Good, dependable, rules. Rules for a balanced, healthy life. Rules his wife *would* follow even though she posed no threat to his heart. She posed other threats, such as driving him mad with her scent and occupying his mind, but not his heart.

He paced the length of his study.

Ambrose never paced.

But threat or no threat, she was part of his family and would be protected as such.

He pinched the bridge of his nose.

He still didn't know his wife's name.

"My dear," "sweetheart," and "honey" were what her family had called her all day, never her name. Ambrose could almost believe she had no name.

His head jerked up when Charles Middleton, his father-in-law, and Bradford Middleton, the Earl of Dashwood, entered his study. He motioned for them to take a seat.

"You are aware of your daughters' actions," Ambrose stated, getting to the point as he sank into the chair behind his desk.

"Hard to miss you marrying the wrong woman," Dashwood drawled.

Ambrose glowered at him before turning to Charles Middleton. "Your daughter breached our betrothal contract."

"My daughters have always been willful," Charles Middleton said in way of agreement. Or apology.

Ambrose wasn't quite sure. "I fear I am to blame for that having indulged them their every whim."

And yet there was no remorse in the man's voice. Not a hint of regret.

"Of course, we will cover any sum of penalty you require," Dashwood said in a business-like manner.

"I don't want your money," Ambrose growled. "I want you to honor the betrothal agreement—except now to my brother, Lord Jonathan."

Both men stiffened.

"Forgive me, Your Grace, but if my daughter did not wish to marry you, she will not wish to wed Lord Jonathan," Charles Middleton said, disapproval etched in his features.

"And yet she did wish to marry me, up until four minutes before the ceremony."

"That does make one wonder, does it not?" Dashwood folded his arms across his chest. "What could have changed my cousin's mind?"

Charles Middleton nodded in accord. "That it does."

A rueful smile curved Ambrose's lips. If they wanted to get a rise out of him, they would wait to eternity. "This is a matter of honor, not what your daughter desires."

"As far as I am concerned, the betrothal agreement has been met," Charles Middleton said. "You wished to marry my daughter and you have. Or am I to understand you have grown fond of Holly?"

"Holly was the name on the betrothal contract," Ambrose said, deadpan.

"St. Ives, let me be frank. I am far too fond of my daughters to be bullied into entering agreements they do not want, or no longer desire to be tied to. As such, if Willow wants an annulment—"

"She will get it when hell freezes over," Ambrose declared, cutting Charles Middleton off. "There will be no annulment."

Willow.

The name suited her.

"If my cousin wants—"

"Your *cousin* married me," Ambrose interrupted, his tone dry as dust. He'd be damned if he annulled this marriage. They could just try to make him. "I'd say she made her choice."

"My daughter may have felt she had no other choice in the matter."

"But she *did* have a choice. And she chose." Ambrose reclined back in his chair. "To annul our marriage now would ruin all three of your daughters."

The man did not even bat an eye. "I already stated I would not be bullied. Make no mistake, St. Ives: if my daughter wishes for an annulment, she will get one, or I will take her away from you, your wrath be damned."

The blood in his head throbbed until Ambrose thought it might implode from the pressure. Dark energy welled inside him, choking him. No one, not her father, not her cousin, not the Royal bloody Regiment, would take his wife from him.

An annulment would reinstate the absurd clause in his father's will but Ambrose feared it was more than that. He did not understand where this sentiment came from exactly, given that he'd planned to ignore his wife after marrying her, but it was there all the same. From the moment he had stared down into her willful blue eyes in the church, her open defiance of her vows, something had sparked to life inside of him. He was keeping his wife. He was keeping Willow—and that was that.

But he said nothing to the men sitting across from him, keeping his face impassive.

"As for betrothing my daughter to Lord Jonathan, I shall consider it as I understand that wrong has been done this day. But I will speak to Holly first."

"And where is your charming," *conniving* "daughter?"

Something shifted in the man's gaze, and all of Ambrose's senses went on alert. *He did not know.*

"I want to know what the hell you did to make my cousin run away from you," Dashwood growled, shifting focus from the topic. "If you hurt her . . ."

Ambrose shot the man a cold look. There were moments in every man's life when his character was tested by his actions—on whether he showed restraint or acted out.

Such a moment was upon Ambrose.

He wanted nothing more than to fly over the desk and lay Dashwood to the ground. But he refrained from the urge, flexing and relaxing his fists. His restraint was why he never thought himself as a browbeating man, even if it was clear these two men thought just that.

All his life he had done what's right—for the most part. It was a point of pride, even though his methods were crusty. His character was beyond reproach. He could control any impulse to the contrary. But he was an imperious man—of that he harbored no delusions.

But the entire situation was damned irritating.

Of course, Ambrose hadn't expected his wife's family to idly sit by, but dash it all to hell! They were supposed to placate him, not tear into him. *He* had been the one jilted. *Their* family had caused the scandal.

"Careful, Dashwood," Ambrose drawled in a tight voice. "There are limits to my tolerance. I have certainly not done anything to warrant a breach of contract."

"But you did do something." Fury flashed in the depth of Dashwood's gaze.

"From where I am sitting, your cousin is the one who did something, not me."

"Holly fled the wedding, presumably from you, and Willow married you. So for whatever bloody reason, you are in the middle of it. I just don't know why."

Ambrose folded his arms over his chest. "Well then, we are all at a loss. Perhaps flaunting convention has finally led to your daughter's actions. But for whatever reason, Holly humiliated my family today. You have my offer of appeasement."

But Dashwood wasn't done. "My cousin may be your wife, but if you hurt her in any way, St. Ives, I will—"

"Do not threaten me, Dashwood," Ambrose growled. "I am not a bastard. I do not harm women."

Dashwood clenched his jaw. The man still wasn't finished. "There are other ways to harm a woman."

Ambrose stiffened. He was a man that could take all manner of insults. He was also used to envious comments and sniping looks, but the one thing he would not—did not—tolerate was being told that he lacked the ability to take care of those in his charge.

"Surely you are not implying I cannot care for my wife?" His words were soft, a challenge.

"There is one thing you ought to know about my cousins, and that is that they are damn resourceful," Dashwood answered.

"What the hell is that supposed to mean?" Ambrose demanded.

Charles Middleton shifted uncomfortably in his seat. It was clear both men expected him to know what Dashwood meant. He was bloody well aware the Middleton chits were crafty. And even if he hadn't been aware of it, today would have proven it. So why were they talking to him in damn riddles?

"I see you don't take my meaning."

"So why don't you enlighten me?" Ambrose snapped, losing patience.

"Your mistress."

That was what this was about?

"And how is that any of your concern?" Ambrose grit out between clenched teeth.

"Cut her loose." Dashwood's eyes blazed.

"Your concern is commendable but let me worry about what reality my wife can and cannot deal with."

He had already broken it off with his mistress, but Dashwood and his pompous nose in his business could go to hell. Just because he married in haste under dubious conditions did not mean he was a complete bastard.

His eyes fell on Charles Middleton and the look on the man's face made him sigh. Ambrose had to give his father-in-law credit, he loved his daughters. "I do possess a strong set of moral principles," he found himself saying against his better judgment. "Having both a wife and a mistress are against them."

"That is good to hear," Charles Middleton said with a nod of approval, relief evident in his features.

Ambrose grunted.

Holly had believed him a beast. And he had been, but he had tried to set it right before the wedding. He had made his deception known when he'd handed her the rules. That was why she had run. It was also what her entire family thought of him, no doubt, even though he was the victim of deception here. Did any of that matter to the Middletons? Of course not. In fact, this was why he had been reluctant to marry all these years. A man did not just acquire a wife in the agreement, he acquired an entire bloody family.

More people to take into account.

More people he could not control.

Now he was more exposed than ever. Everything had gone wrong. And he was in possession of a wife that had a big question mark behind her name. What did he know of her? Except she was fiercely loyal to her family and did as she pleased.

Ambrose bit back a curse. The last thing he wanted to feel for his wife was admiration. If he felt that, who knew what other things he might come to feel, what other emotions would sneak up on him.

Damn that kiss. Something deep, dark, and ravenous had awoken inside him when their lips had met, a sensation he did not care to delve deeper into.

Ambrose was pulled from his thoughts when Charles Middleton stood, Dashwood following suit. "I believe we have said all we have come to say. I will send word once I've reached a decision."

Ambrose nodded, rising from behind his desk. "I ask only that Miss Middleton remain with my wife and I until your final decision has been made."

"Uncle," Dashwood warned, opposed to the idea.

"Do I have your word that you will not marry her off without my consent?" Charles Middleton asked.

"You do."

"Then she can stay in your care for the time being, if that is what she desires."

Ambrose was no fool. That was not what Holly desired, which was why she was long gone. Charles Middleton was aware of that. The man knew as much of his daughter's whereabouts as Ambrose did. But he'd received the permission he needed should his men find her.

Dashwood shot him a scathing glare before turning on his heel and marching out, Charles Middleton following suit at a slower pace.

As soon as they were gone, Ambrose dropped back in his seat, dragging a hand through his hair. What the hell did he do now? Drink? Search out his wife? Confront her? Consummate the marriage before she changed her mind? He had meant what he said. He would not annul the marriage, regardless of whether it had been consummated or not.

Which it damn well would be.

And perhaps it had been wishful thinking on his part that his life would remain unchanged now that a wife occupied the walls of his home, slept in the room adjoining his.

She would be so close. Even now he imagined listening to the soft padding of her footsteps as she settled in for the night. He would rather not think of her laying her head on a bed of pillows, breathing, stretching out her lithe body.

Nothing was supposed to change. He wasn't supposed to be plagued by thoughts of his wife. Especially since she was never meant to be his wife. And yet it was impossible not to wonder what she was feeling at that moment. Was she angry? Scared? Did she feel invincible?

Ambrose loathed change. Ever since Celia became sick all those years ago, change always made him antsy. And more often than not, when changed occurred, Ambrose needed to reassess his limits, his environment. And breathe.

Breathe.

The study was too stuffy. He couldn't think here, knowing somewhere in the house, in her chamber, his wife waited for him. All he wanted was to go back to his life the way it was twelve months ago. No complications. No commitments. No doubt and uncertainty festering in his belly.

But as if the day could not get any worse, Quinn Middleton entered, his eyes smoldering. Murderous, even.

Ambrose sighed.

There would be no reprieve for him apparently.

"What the hell do you want?" Ambrose snapped, losing some of his composure. "Your brethren have already voiced their grievances."

"But I have not." Quinn's face hardened to stone. "Do not think I won't take Willow away from you if I suspect my cousin is unhappy."

"If you ever take my wife away from me, pup, I will see you dealt with in ways you cannot fathom." His voice was low, laced with malice. Promise.

He was tired of people threatening to remove his wife from his life.

The man's shoulders bunched at the threat. "Don't mistake me for one of your saplings, St. Ives. If you hurt my cousin, there *will* be hell to pay."

A sardonic smile stretched across Ambrose's lips. *Well, so much for welcoming family in-laws.* With one last parting glare, in which Ambrose just raised his brows at the pup, Quinn Middleton stalked from the room, shouldering past Jonathan, who appeared just then in the threshold.

"Who the hell did you piss off now?" Jonathan muttered, striding into the room and dropping down in a chair. "Christ, my head is throbbing."

"Where the hell have you been?" Ambrose demanded.

"Dammit man, must you yell?"

"Where have you been?" Ambrose insisted with a glower. "Your presence was required today."

Jonathan rolled his eyes. "If you must know, I was at Hazard's all night."

"The gaming hell?"

Jonathan nodded. "Having the time of my life."

"*You missed my wedding for a damn night on the town?*" Ambrose practically roared.

"What?" Jonathan shot upright. "No! That's not until the sixteenth!"

"Today is the sixteenth!"

"The hell you say!" But Jonathan's pallor was already replaced by an unpleasant shade of pink.

Ambrose scrubbed his face with his hands. "Unbelievable."

Jonathan slowly sat back down, shame written on his face. "I missed your wedding, didn't I?"

"It's done now," Ambrose muttered, falling back into his chair, his eyes shutting.

What was done was done. His brother had been recovering from a night of gambling and indulgence while he had been deserted by his betrothed and married her sister. His mother was beside herself and his in-laws despised him.

And he didn't know a damn thing about his new wife.

He let out a heavy sigh.

Ambrose could not help but wonder if today marked defining moments for them all.

Chapter 6

Willow sank down on her bed and then immediately jumped back up. Nerves ate away at her belly as she waited for her husband to make his entrance. There were a few things they needed to discuss. Such as expectations. Holly. The reason he wished to wed in haste.

Her gaze wandered over to the sheets of paper neatly arranged on her desk.

Boundaries for the Duchess of St. Ives.

Willow huffed.

The title *had* a well-defined ring to it, but the document itself represented everything she stood against. Of course, she had been raised without many restrictions, skirting around the edges of what was proper and what was not. She had grown up with freedom few women possessed, a way of life she had perhaps taken for granted.

Willow had always assumed her husband would possess the same values as her father. It never occurred to her he may not. Then again, it never occurred to her that she would come to be married in the way she did. There had not been much time dedicated to considering the character of her husband. Well, not much beyond the idea that she would be able to manage the duke.

Boundaries.

Hah! What did that even mean? A clear line drawn across the floor of their home? That might not be such a terrible idea. Certainly not after that kiss which had, in the blink of a second, tested the purely beastly view Willow had constructed of the duke. The kiss alone suggested there was something underneath the beast, a man that could feel.

His rigid need for control certainly did not paint a man who possessed such a passionate side. It had thrown her off balance. In fact, Willow had to remind herself over and over that her husband was reputed to be a stuffy duke. It was dangerous to imagine him as anything romantic. He wasn't. He had tricked Holly and drawn up these rules.

Willow must remember that.

And just what did he mean to gain from setting up such absurd rules as eating one meager piece of toast in the morning? Was it perhaps a miracle slice of bread? That had been the worst rule for Holly.

She glared at the offending sheets of paper.

She ought to read them. But she wouldn't. The mere thought of it stuck in her craw.

Her fingers skimmed over the title.

As long as she remained unaware of the contents, there was a chance for her to form her own opinions about her husband. If she read the rules and became infuriated, they would not get off to any sort of start and for better or worse, they were married. Besides, she had no intention of following his ridiculous rules. She fully planned to ignore the "boundaries" he had drawn up for her. If they were so important to him, the man could very well explain why himself!

She cast an irritable glance at the door.

She wondered what kind of entrance he would make. Would he burst into the chamber tall, handsome and naked? Or would he expect her to undress him? Perhaps he was a robe man.

Willow sighed at herself. One minute she was fuming over his boundary book and the next she was imagining him naked. It was more than confusing.

She had attempted all day–ever since his kiss—*not* to imagine her husband naked. Which was proving quite impossible. Whenever he moved, the roped muscles of his body rippled in such a delicious way, tremors tormented her spine.

She didn't think she'd mind consummating the marriage one bit. At least in this, she didn't feel torn.

She quelled the tiny pinch of guilt that surfaced at the thought of why she married him. She ought not feel guilty. Her actions weren't any different from men acquiring wives to beget them an heir, was it?

The sudden thud of polished Hessians in the hallway caused her pulse to leap. Alert, she listened as her husband entered his chambers, the door groaning on its hinges as it shut. The soft rustle of fabric that soon followed.

Her eyes shot to the door adjoining their rooms.

She tried to remember why she was annoyed, what she planned on demanding explanations for, when all of a sudden, she couldn't even catch her breath, let alone think.

Butterflies fluttered wildly in her belly. *Think, Willow. Think!* But the doorknob turned and her wits scattered. Her blood throbbed in her veins. She waited in suspended time for the door to push open.

But . . . nothing.

Her brows puckered.

The doorknob wiggled again.

"Open the door, Willow."

The door was locked?

Then, a moment later, realization sunk in. Had he just called her—

"Willow."

There it was again, the soft purr of her name. Which rolling off his tongue sounded like sweet honey dripping from his lips when he pronounced it.

She shuddered.

And just like that, panic set in. What had she been thinking! She married her sister's jilted betrothed to get with child! She'd lost her mind. Her reasoning was flawed. And how did she think that she would enjoy the consummation? She didn't even know what it entailed! She belonged in Bedlam!

On instinct, she dashed to the bedroom door and yanked it open, resolved to hide away in the servant quarters or behind a curtain somewhere, just for the night, and bolted straight into a broad chest.

Strong arms circled her waist and crushed her against a hard frame while walking her back into the room. Her head tilted back to meet the dark, smoldering eyes of her husband, wicked amusement flashing in their surface.

"Going somewhere?"

She bit her bottom lip. "I, er, no, I . . ." Willow trailed off, breathless.

"Not running away from your husband, then?" he mocked. "It must be a family trait."

"Of course not," Willow scoffed, feeling more herself when her temper sparked.

He chuckled, setting her back on her feet, kicking the door shut. "Little liar."

"I see you recalled my name?" Willow remarked, choosing to ignore his devilish expression.

"Indeed." He smiled then, a look so dazzling she hastily backed away, nearly stumbling over a footstool. He reached out to steady her.

She blinked a few times to ensure she was not dreaming. Her husband stood in the centre of her chamber in nothing but a robe. He *was* a robe man. And she was acting like a nitwit at the sight of it. Which was why, of course, she said the first thing that popped into her brain, anything to keep her mind from the flush spreading up her neck and the quickening beat of her heart.

"Well, *Ambrose*, you ought to know, I will have at least three pieces of toast in the morning."

For a moment, confusion shone in his features and then his eyes narrowed. "If you read the—"

"I did not read that pile of rubbish," Willow motioned at the papers on her desk, "I heard this particular *rule* from my sister and I'm making it clear that I will not be following it."

She stepped right up to him, daring him to contradict her. She could feel the heat coming off his body and struggled to ignore its beckoning. What sort of wanton creature was she? And the feelings he aroused in her just served to set fire to the glowing embers of her annoyance. She was feeling all sorts of things she ought not to feel. And yet for all her annoyance, she felt *awakened*.

His jaw tightened, but his mask of amusement did not slip.

"Willow, the rules are—"

"Preposterous, I imagine."

"Stop interrupting me when I'm trying—"

"To say you agree with me?"

Finally, anger flashed across his features, cracking through his good-humor. She felt satisfaction trill through her.

"Deuce take it! I am trying to protect you," he ground out.

She smiled up at him sweetly. "From toast?"

A low growl rumbled deep in his throat. It was her only warning. Hunger, starkly raw, flashed in his eyes before he brought his mouth down on hers. There was nothing gentle about the kiss, though nothing bruising. But it didn't matter. Because the moment he touched her lips, flames lapped up her skin.

Everything she'd been holding back, everything she'd been fighting to ignore overwhelmed her. Fear, annoyance, guilt, and desire all poured out in the kiss. Their locked horns became something else as their tongues dueled. And she recalled that his purpose for being here, in her chamber, in this moment, was another one altogether different from negotiations over toast.

Suddenly, he pulled away, and Willow found herself stunned and bereft. Her eyes opened to find him shrugging off his robe in one smooth motion, allowing it to fall to the ground in a crumpled heap.

Willow nearly choked on air.

"You're . . . you're . . ."

He was completely, splendidly and breathtakingly naked.

Willow backed away from him, her lips parting as her gaze wandered over every sinew that rippled across his torso. His thick muscles thrummed with strength.

He stalked her with a slow gait, the motion drawing her gaze lower.

Her eyes snapped back up again. "You cannot possibly waltz into my bedchamber naked and all . . . all . . . . naked!"

But he could.

And he did.

He arched a bemused brow. "No?"

"You cannot possibly mean to . . ." her words tapered off on a breathless note.

But he could.

And he meant to.

She saw it in the gleam of his eyes and realized she wanted to do . . . whatever he wanted.

"A good wife would have been naked by now, not arguing with me about breakfast."

Willow flushed scarlet. She wouldn't admit that breakfast was presently the furthest thing from her mind. She could easily win that argument in the morning. There were more pressing matters at the moment, matters she was rather entranced by. Naked matters. Husband matters. *Consummation* matters.

"Are you under the impression that wives lounged nude in wait for their husbands all day?" She sniffed in mock disdain. "They do not."

His lips pulled back in a smile. "If they did, no man would ever leave their bed."

"Men tire easily enough."

"Not all men."

The words, the rough baritone of his voice, brought a shiver to her spine.

Did he mean himself? That the thought thrilled her made it clear: her sanity was, indeed, lost. Because the thought of lounging around naked waiting on the duke sounded ridiculously delightful.

"So what is it to be, wife?"

"I beg your pardon?" Her eyes, which were busy examining his torso, jerked up to his face.

"I'm all for hiking your skirts up and consummating this marriage without delay, though I'd rather it be your choice." His eyes raked her up and down, gaze blazing. "And I'd rather you be naked."

"You are allowing me the chance to decline?"

He shrugged. "But be warned, little wife, this marriage will not be annulled. I will have your word."

Dear lord, he was giving her a way out of their wedding night. And he truly thought she would seize the chance. Willow glimpsed it there, in the amusement of his features, his flashing eyes.

"So?" he pressed.

Wicked scoundrel! Challenge wove through the threads of his words. He must want this marriage badly. She made a mental note to demand answers later.

At present, however, it seemed she loved battling with him as much as she loved looking at him. Indeed, she found herself wanting to explore their wedding night more than anything in that moment. Thus, Willow gave him something better than her word.

She turned and gave him her back. "Unlace me."

Her boldness amazed her. Empowered her. Then she felt the caress of his hand brushing her neck followed by the soft graze of his lips against her skin. Her lashes drifted shut.

"Are you certain?" His velvety voice whispered in her ear.

Heat pooled in her belly. Breathless, she answered, "Yes."

Three heartbeats later, her dress pooled around her feet. Seconds later, her petticoat, chemise and stays followed.

She heard him suck in his breath.

Emboldened by his response, and seeing no point in holding onto modesty, Willow turned and brazenly met her husband's gaze. The impact was so strong the air rushed from her lungs. His eyes were intense. More intense than usual. And the way he was staring at her singed skin.

Her tongue darted over her lower lip. He reached for her, drawing her against the hard ridges of his body and then he was kissing her again. All at once, she was lifted up into his arms.

Willow barely had time to soak up the delightful heat of his skin. Dropping her on the bed, his eyes were warm as they searched hers.

She liked his eyes this way—warm, expressive—and wondered what it would take to keep them so.

"Earlier, when you were running for the door . . . you wanted to escape me." His voice was low. Seductive. He stretched over her, covering her with his entire masculine length. "Did you not?"

"I'll admit to no such thing," Willow muttered, her wits scrambled. It was hard to draw a thought with him this close.

His chest rumbled with laughter and he pinned her with ruthless, glowing eyes. His face could have been etched in stone at that moment. The breath in her lungs burned. But the answer he sought was there in her eyes—she never once thought she could escape him.

The look of sheer male satisfaction that crossed his features ought to have raised the hairs on her neck but his lips lowered to slide over her collarbone, skimming breasts, her belly, burning through her annoyance. Nowhere was off limits. Fire spread through her.

The hard contrast of his muscles against her softness made Willow's head spin. Without warning, his hand settled at the junction of her legs and she yelped, not expecting his dexterous fingers to make such a play.

"Relax," he murmured before his fingers continued their exploration. His eyes locked on hers as sensations rocked through her, radiating out from her core. "Did you not think about this when you chose to walk down the church?"

No, absolutely not had she thought about what his hands might do.

"Or this?" His finger disappeared, only to be replaced by his mouth.

Lud no, she had not imagined that either.

When his tongue flicked over the folds of her core, Willow whimpered. It was just so wicked. She may die from delight. Or embarrassment. Or something. Yet he seemed not at all ashamed by what he was doing.

He continued until she thought she might explode. She writhed beneath him wildly, impatient. With a quiet laugh, he lifted himself up and surrounded her with his body, his hands and mouth on her breasts, her neck, his throbbing member pushing at her entrance.

"This may hurt," he said, his voice hoarse.

Hurt?

Nothing could ever hurt again. It seemed most ridiculous for him to say that. She was riding in a haze of pleasure.

He surged forward, driving past her innocence.

"Dear lord," she cried out, nearly bulking from the bed at the unexpected pain. "You could have warned me."

"I did," he bit out but sounded amused.

She writhed beneath him and he groaned, noting his clenched jaw. "Is it painful for you, too?"

He shook his head.

"Then why have you stopped?"

His eyes bore into hers. "To give you time to adjust to me."

Oh!

She tested another wiggle. "It doesn't hurt anymore."

His lips descended on hers and he began to thrust into her, low, firm movements that set fire to her insides. This time, Willow did not hold back. She stroked her tongue alongside his, tasting, feasting. She felt wild inside, and gave herself over to her husband's attention, his thrusts, to the flames licking up her spine. This was so much more than she had ever expected.

If this was part of what it meant to be a wife, Willow thought, she'd happily do this as often as possible.

Lifting her hips to meet each of his thrusts, his name slipped from her lips. There was something precious happening between them, something magical.

His movements gained more purpose, and she arched her back, pleasure exploding inside her like a thousand stars bursting into stardust. Moments later, he shuddered his own release, his body a delightful weight pressing into her.

"That was marvelous," Willow said once she caught her breath.

One corner of his mouth quirked up. "Indeed," he agreed, rolling onto his back.

"I had no idea that it could be so . . ." her voice trailed off at a loss for words. Her imagination had not prepared her for the emotions his touch provoked. The ethereal feeling that her body no longer belonged to her.

He turned his head to her. "How did it feel?"

"Earth-shattering," she said, meeting his gaze.

"That's good," he said. "Perhaps tomorrow you can read through the rules I have—"

"I'm not reading your rules," Willow cut him off, bolting upright to glare at him.

His eyes hardened. "Wives do as they are told."

"Not this wife," she declared, indignant.

"Then you will not feel that *earth-shattering* pleasure again."

Willow gasped. Ice water could not have been more effective. She scrambled away from him, grabbing the sheets to cover herself. Furious and pained all at once.

"Was this all a trap? Seduce me so I'll be more biddable?"

"No," he said, sitting up. "I gave you a choice to consummate this marriage or give me your word it will not be annulled."

Dear lord, he was right. She had wanted this, all of it. But she hadn't expected he'd introduce her to such exquisite passion and then threaten to take it away.

"That's . . . that's . . . deplorable!" Willow exploded. "How can you threaten me like this after what we shared?"

His eyes were once again frosty. "Oh, I can, my sweet wife. You should understand I am not a man to attach any romantic ideals to."

He'd ruined this marvelous night over *toast*? Well, not actual toast, but rather a metaphor for his obnoxious rules and her refusal to follow them.

"And what if I seek pleasure elsewhere?" Willow challenged, her temper rising at the utter audacity of the man. She wouldn't, but she was furious that he'd crushed a spectacular moment, that he'd reverted them back to their battle of wills. Of course, she'd planned to do the same thing in the morning, but not *now*.

"I would not test me that way if I were you." Black eyes darkened to resemble a thunderstorm. "Not if you do not wish to be locked away in a remote castle on abandoned moors for the rest of your life."

"You wouldn't!"

He only smiled.

Willow watched, crippled with astonishment, as he rose from the bed and padded over to his room with no modesty whatsoever, turning the key in the lock to unlock the door. He did not so much as spare her a second glance!

Glaring at his back, she tossed a pillow at him, but it connected with the wall. The devil with him and his threats so nonchalantly declared! The man was a beast. An appealing beast, but a beast all the same.

And she was just the woman to tame him.

Ambrose cursed a string of foul oaths as he slammed the adjoining door shut. He was supposed to remain detached and stoic. He was supposed to be a master at it. What the hell, then, had happened? Where had all the years of control gone?

In the short time he'd spent with his wife, he'd felt desire, fury, possession, protectiveness, jealously, pleasure, and even—he couldn't comprehend it—affection. He hadn't actually thought she'd go through with the wedding night. He had gone to her chamber fully intending to disrobe and fully expecting her swift word that the marriage would not be annulled.

He wasn't even sure why he had given her the choice, only that it seemed right. And yes, while he had meant for the marriage to be one of convenience, there had been nothing convenient about what had just happened. His world had been pushed over a ravine and was now careening down into some unknown abyss.

Never had he known such raw hunger for a woman. The anger that had burned inside him all day had transformed into wild lust the moment his wife faced him, eyes flashing with defiance, and declared she refused to follow his rules. And then she turned and asked him to unlace her.

The memory still burned against his skull.

With a groan, he fell back on the mattress, staring at the canopy of his bed. He had planned on treating his wife with detachment and distance. But tonight his control had snapped. Just snapped. As if it was nothing more than a thin piece of centuries old rope.

The thought rightly terrified him.

Ambrose needed the ever-present constant of what control provided in his life. Predictability. Routine. Not bloody surprises lurking around each corner. Or underneath petticoats.

He rose to his feet and sauntered over to the window, pulling another robe over his shoulders. The moon had slid behind a cloud, casting gloomy darkness over Mayfair. He lifted a trembling hand—trembling, for Christ's sake—watching the moonlight play over his fingers with a scowl. If he had been in a mood to summon up any form of humor, he'd have laughed for being so unsettled over a woman.

Denial, however, was a waste of his time. Tonight had disturbed him. His wife disturbed him.

But he could not help his mind returning to the memory of how she'd come undone in his arms.

Confusion swamped him.

Why hadn't that been enough? Didn't that make a point about who was in charge?

It should've, but it hadn't.

He hadn't felt in control in the slightest. It was as if, on hearing her pleasure, on seeing her satisfaction, he panicked. And in his panic, he slammed his mask on and tossed out a challenge—said anything to prevent her from looking at him with affection, with hope.

And it had worked. Fury and shock had overtaken her softer emotions instantly.

But bloody hell. What was he getting himself into? He'd incited a war. War was not *detached.*

A movement drew his attention to the shadows where a slight contour flitted over the garden. His eyes narrowed on the silhouette, certain he was hallucinating. But sure enough, a slender figure dashed over the lawn and down the street.

Everything inside him ceased to function.

His gaze ripped away from the window to his wife's chamber and before he could even blink, he threw open the adjoining door. Rage exploded in him, throbbed at his temples. The bed was empty, as was the chamber.

His gaze swept to the open window. Anger choked him. Had the bloody woman been idiotic enough to climb down the window?

It was two stories up!

This, *this*, right here was why he required control in his life. Because once control slipped and the woman in your life ran rampant, nightmarish things happened. God only knows what she was up to—though he suspected it had to do with Holly Middleton. God knew whether she would be safe. He didn't even know where she might have gone. He was powerless to protect her should trouble happen upon her.

How the hell was he supposed to manage an unmanageable wife?

Reason? Threaten? Command? *Beg*?

He stomped back into his room and sank down onto the bed to wait. His mind raced, considering what to do about his wife. Kissing her had been a huge mistake, and he could not repeat it. He had to keep his distance, remain detached. Detachment allowed him the best control.

So Ambrose waited and waited until he heard the tell-tale sound of the floorboards creaking, signaling her return. Only then did he let loose a breath and climb into bed, still no wiser as to how to handle the new Duchess of St. Ives.

Chapter 7

Willow scaled down the side of her new home with little effort—it was a skill she and her sisters perfected when they were twelve years old. Her new home was built in much the same way their country house was, and the distance from this chamber to the ground was not at all different from her chamber in Derbyshire.

The only real difference in this particular house was that it housed a most suspicious, arrogant, misguided male, who would try to stop her. So for that reason, she tried to keep her grunts and heaving to a minimum.

She dropped to the ground with an easy thud, her chin lifting to gaze back up to her window. She wouldn't be able to make it back up again. And there was no tree near her window she could climb. She would have to find another way inside or slip in when the servants woke.

If her husband learned of it, he'd be furious.

Willow shrugged.

Oh well.

What would he next threaten to deny her if he learned about this? The sour cur!

Well, he'd learn. She could live without that pleasure. In fact, she could live without a great deal many things if his seed had taken root. Indeed, if tonight had accomplished her goal, then she'd be the one to withhold rocking *his* world.

See how he enjoys that!

One thing she was not about to do was give up all her dignity and let him plow away for his own pleasure. She wasn't that desperate. If she was not with child . . . Then she would wait until she and Ambrose were on more agreeable terms.

Nevertheless, she was curious to see just how serious he was about his declaration. She needed to take stock of his word, push the boundaries, and discover what sort of character her husband possessed and work from there.

With a resolved nod, she dashed across the lawn.

The thudding of her boots against the cold cobblestones kept her on high alert. It had been less challenging to slip out than she first thought. Right before her sister had departed, Poppy mentioned that the duke planned on stationing footman at her door, or so it was rumored, and Willow hadn't wanted to take the chance to slip out that way. But even in choosing to go out the window, part of her had expected to be caught in the garden.

Keeping her head low and her cloak tightly wound, she spied Warton's carriage in the distance. The footman spotted her and jumped from his perch to open the door.

She gave a curt nod in acknowledgment.

"Milady," he nodded back, ushering her inside—all very cloak and dagger.

Willow found herself peeking through the window every two seconds, half expecting her husband to give chase on the back of a fire breathing dragon. Or God forbid, follow from a discreet distance and catch her in the act of meeting with Holly.

Luckily, the ride to Warton's residence did not take long.

But it wasn't until Willow stood across from Holly in Warton's drawing room that her heart settled back into a steady rhythm.

"Holly?" Willow murmured, her voice cracking just a bit.

Then her sister was in her arms, drawing her into a tight embrace.

Tears gathered in Willow's eyes as she fought to regain some control over her emotions, which appeared to be scattered all over the British Isles. The weight of the day's events bore down hard on her heart, as did the fear that her sister may be angry with her and even feel betrayed by her actions.

"I thought I wouldn't see you before we left," Holly murmured.

"Nothing could keep me away," Willow said, drawing back to take a good look at her sister. "However, my husband made it slightly more difficult when he supposedly stationed two footmen outside my bedchamber. To keep me in or to keep you out, who is to say? It seems he does not believe I would risk scaling down the side of a house to see you."

"Forgive me, Willow. If I'd known you would do something so insane in an attempt to correct my imprudence, I would never have left you alone in that room. Was he furious with you?"

"Oh, he was quite beyond that, but nothing I couldn't manage. The Dragon Duchess, as you so suitably named her, on the other hand . . ." Willow shuddered. "That woman's wailing almost drove me through the walls. Her incessant caterwauling gave me head pains. She needs to take to the waters of Bath."

"I am so sorry."

Her sister appeared truly torn up by the events, as though she was to blame. When in fact, the choice had been Willow's. And she did not regret it. Well, maybe a tiny bit after tonight. Clearly, she hadn't understood what she was marrying into or she might have run faster than Holly had. Maybe. But she was in this marriage now and had to make the most of it. Middletons did not give up.

"Oh, hush, I would never have allowed you to marry that beast, not after what you told me. Besides, I have my own motivation for wedding the man."

"You *wanted* to marry St. Ives?"

"Of course not. My reasons have nothing to do with the duke himself."

"I am confused. The reason you married him has nothing to do with him?"

"Yes," Willow said with a slow nod, her heart jumping into her throat.

"But the man is a beast," Holly pointed out, a worried look flittering across her face.

"He is something, all right," Willow murmured, giving her a soft, reassuring smile. And while it was certainly an infuriating something most of the time, Willow also had to admit that the "something" also included a peculiar presence. An aura surrounded the duke that Willow felt drawn to—and she was certainly attracted to the man given their most recent interaction.

But she couldn't admit any of this to her sister. Holly had been in love with St. Ives mere days ago.

"I believe what your sister is saying, Miss Middleton," Warton spoke up, his eyes resting on Holly, "is that she wished to marry and took advantage of an available groom."

Holly's gaze flew to Willow. "Is that true?"

Willow nodded, relieved that Warton had so easily come to the right conclusion. She gave her sister a sheepish smile. "But please know I never intended on stealing your betrothed before that moment."

"I suppose that is a comforting thought," Holly said, her eyes sparkling. Then just as suddenly, her amusement faded. "Has St. Ives spoken to father yet?"

Willow nodded, allowing Holly to tug her to the sofa.

"So, does father mean to lock me away in a tower or perhaps, dare I ask, a dungeon?"

It would be just like her sister to find that thought most intriguing! "I'm afraid not. The duke has requested father's permission to establish a betrothal agreement for you and his brother, Lord Jonathan Griffin."

"I must not have heard you correctly, Willow, because it sounded like you said the duke wants me to marry his *brother*?"

Willow gave her a solemn look.

"I cannot marry your brother-in-law, I do not love him!"

"Regardless of anyone's feelings, St. Ives has men searching every inch of the city. He suspects, or at least I think he does, that you might return to Derbyshire. He has already dispatched men there, as well."

"But why? Lord Jonathan is on tour. He even missed the wedding."

"He is expected back any day now, I'm afraid."

"Surely Lord Jonathan will not stand for this?"

"I thought so as well, but what if the duke threatened to cut his brother off?"

"He could marry an heiress."

"It will still require him to marry. So why not marry you and keep his brother happy?"

"Has father agreed to this arrangement?"

"Not as of yet."

"Well, then, St. Ives must have demanded father agree, and Lord knows father hates to be told what to do."

"No man does," Warton muttered from behind them.

Holly let out a small sigh. "Is it not a crime to wed a relation by marriage?" she asked.

"Unfortunately not," Willow said. It would have made things much easier.

"A pity."

Willow gave her sister's hand a reassuring squeeze. "I won't let it come to that. But it might be best if you put some distance between you and the city."

A lot of distance.

"The marquis has agreed to escort me to one of his properties in—"

Willow held up her hand, stopping Holly midsentence. "Do not tell me where you are going. I don't want to take the chance of spilling your whereabouts, however unintentional." She glanced at Warton, considering him a moment.

He was a man of passionate temper, but a gentleman of honor. They made quite the pair, these two. Almost like pork and apples, an odd combination, but somehow the flavors worked. "What of your servants? Are they aware of your destination?"

"I assure you, madam," Warton drawled, "my servants do not gossip."

How utterly male of him to assume that.

"Servants gossip among each other, if nothing else," Willow pointed out. "And you've given yours the night off in the wake of a huge scandal. They may not realize the significance, but others may draw suspicion from that."

"Point taken," Warton grumbled.

Willow suppressed a smile. She wondered what could have driven Warton to help Holly. It wasn't precisely in line with his reputation or character. The man was a well-known grump. By all accounts, the marquis ought to have dragged Holly back to their father and washed his hands of her, not dive straight into the hornet's nest.

Was there something more to it than simply help? He was difficult to read, but she noticed how he always seemed to keep his eyes on Holly. That, if nothing else, would likely keep her out of trouble.

And Willow trusted Warton.

"We shall be careful to remain undetected," Holly reassured.

Willow nodded. "Stop only where you are confident no one will recognize you. For the time being, the duke doesn't suspect you have a protector. That gives you an advantage, Holly, so use it wisely. I will do what I can from here, but we must think of an alternative plan in case I fail to convince the duke to let the matter go."

"No one will catch us off guard," Warton griped.

"Thank you." Willow knew she needed to assure him that they were all grateful for his aiding Holly. "I owe you a great debt for aiding my sister."

He grunted. "The duke will not get his hands on her."

Willow turned to her sister, one brow arched. She said with her eyes what she could not speak out loud with Warton within earshot: *Now is not the time to fall in love with this man.*

Holly shrugged noncommittally and Willow fought the urge to huff out in frustration. She adored her sister, but Holly was too quick to fall head over heels.

"How will you appeal to St. Ives to accept an olive branch?"

"I have no clue, but I shall figure something out. The man is as stubborn as an ox, intent on dictating the lives of others. It shall give me great pleasure to bring him down a notch or two."

"He has not hurt you?"

Willow heard the fear in Holly's tone, but she truly didn't think that her husband was that kind of man. He would've shown those colors already if he was. Instead, he'd threatened to deny her pleasure. Intolerable behavior, certainly, but she felt that his "rules" and "boundaries" were the worst of it.

"No, dear, I do not believe he shall. He seeks only to control me, and I daresay, should he discover me gone, it will give him quite the fit! But that's the most of it."

"You are so terrible, Willow," Holly said with a smile. "Best hope he does not realize you are gone."

"It might do him some good to discover his wife is in possession of a fine backbone."

"I cannot express enough how sorry I am," Holly murmured.

"Stop apologizing," Willow demanded. She glanced at Warton. "I came to see if you were all right, and I am pleased to find you have chanced upon a champion of sorts, however shocking."

Warton lifted one dark brow.

"Well, it is," Willow reaffirmed. "If I penned down all of the *least* likely gentlemen to aid my sister, you would have been on the top of that list."

"And why is that, Duchess?"

"Oh, you are known to have a brooding temperament and a quick temper. Not to mention you lack the subtle charm that most gentlemen possess."

"I have charm," he muttered.

Holly was clearly smothering a smile. "I'm sure Warton regrets the curiosity that led him to stumble upon me," she teased.

Willow glanced between the two. Warton only grunted in response, but the small pull of his lips told Willow he found their remarks amusing. But the smile her sister sent his way was more than mere gratefulness.

Willow knew her sister well, had spent a lifetime learning the small expressions that gave away the beginning of an infatuation. This was one of them.

Willow's brow puckered. She felt it her sisterly duty to advise against any infatuations for the time being. "Please do not accept another proposal before the dust has settled."

The slight color of Holly's cheeks turned molten. "Do not be silly; I have no wish to fall into the same trap again. And I doubt there's a man in England who would ask for my hand after today," she muttered in a hushed tone. "In any case, I'm practically betrothed to Lord Jonathan Griffin now, am I not?"

"You are not betrothed yet, and with any luck, you won't be. Best not to provoke St. Ives further until this matter with his brother is resolved."

"Do not worry; I shall not fall in love on a whim again."

Willow stifled a snort. She hoped so. But mostly she hoped that if her sister did fall in love again, it would not be with the wrong man this time—and it would be lasting rather than fleeting.

"That is all I ask," Willow murmured. "In any event, I can see that you are in capable hands. Come, I must be off."

"So soon?"

Willow gave a reluctant nod in reply. She knew she'd already been absent long enough.

"Take care of my sister," she told Warton. "The next time we meet, I hope it will be under better circumstances."

Warton inclined his head.

That he was her sister's reluctant champion was truly remarkable in itself, Willow thought once again. The Marquis was known for his low tolerance for silly antics, and the Middleton sisters were often synonymous with silly—at least in the past.

"Be well," Holly murmured.

She planned on being just that. Beyond relieved her sister was safe and happy, Willow could now shift her attention toward her husband.

Anticipation rippled along her spine. She should be furious—and part of her still was—but she was thrilled, as well. She planned on peeling away the layers of the duke until she found the man beneath the mask.

Who would've guessed she loved sparing with her testy duke so much?

Chapter 8

A soft noise drew Willow from her slumber. She lifted her lashes slowly. Light blazed through the window. Hadn't she closed the curtains upon her return? Groaning, she delved deeper into the covers, seeking sleep. But there it was again, a slight rustle that she couldn't quite pinpoint. With a mental sigh, Willow poked her head from the covers, her eyes searching for the disturbance.

Her gaze moved to the window, which was open, a light breeze pushing at the curtains. That must be it. Willow's head fell back on the pillows, her lashes resting once more on her cheeks. She could have sworn she'd closed the window last night. She must have been quite exhausted.

"I see you are awake."

Willow's eyes shot open.

The low drawl of her husband's voice snapped her out of her drowsiness and she lurched upright, her eyes locking with the hard crystals of the duke's.

He stood—too damn handsome for his own good—at the edge of the bed, looming over her. His dark eyes hot and furious.

How long has he been standing there, watching her sleep?

Willow blinked up at him, her hand lifting to pat her mass of tangled bed hair. She always looked a fright in the morning.

He arched a brow.

Someone was in a mood this morning!

"Is something amiss?" Willow murmured, pulling the covers up to her chin. She tried to ignore the thin line of his lips, the hard edge of his jaw.

Had she slept in too late? Had she broken one of his precious rules? Willow almost snorted. She would rise when she was right and ready—which wasn't at this moment.

She arched a brow right back at him.

He continued to glare at her in silence.

How she wished he was less beautiful. At the very least, it would have made his deplorable disposition easier to ignore. She couldn't very well ignore his moods if she couldn't stop staring at his face. And she certainly did *not* want to stare at his face. She'd rather stare at his lips, truth be told.

So she did.

They were much better to stare at anyway. They did not *glare*. They were full and tempting. And probably tasted of coffee.

"Do you find something fascinating on my face?"

Willow's lashes lifted to meet piercing eyes. "Have I broken one of your precious rules while sleeping?"

His eyes narrowed, flicking to the untouched set of papers on her desk. "You would know if you had bothered to read them."

"I already told you, I'm not much of a reader."

"Then I shall read them to you," he ground out.

"I'm not much of a listener, either."

His shoulders tensed, the veins in his neck were thick and visible. But Willow did not acknowledge his temper and instead, had to bite back a groan at the sight of him all furious. All it did was remind her of last night, of his hands and mouth all over her body, attacking her senses.

Oh dear Lord, was she lusting after her husband?

In her defense, she hadn't expected their wedding night to be so marvelous. She wanted more of it. Lots more. But at the same time, she could not allow this man to rule her with a set of dictates. Not even for the pleasure that likely came with it.

She was a rule flaunter, after all.

Still, a tinge of fear hovered on the surface of that thought. Fear that she may fail to help her sister. Fear that *he* would succeed in making her miserable. Fear this war would last for the rest of her life and they'd find no common ground.

She dashed the thought from her mind. Defeat was not something Willow was willing to contemplate. Not ever.

"Not being much of a reader or listener, I suppose you excel at other things—like wandering off on midnight strolls?"

Ah.

Willow swore her chest cracked open, her heart beat so wildly. She rose to a seated position.

"I never took midnight strolling for a skill," she murmured. Might as well go down in blazing sarcasm.

"Where the hell did you go last night?"

"To bed?"

The edges of his lips tightened. "Do not mock me. Last night after I left, you snuck out to see *her*."

Willow squared her shoulders. The way he spat the word had her hackles rising. "This *her* you refer to—"

"Where is she?" he pressed.

"I cannot possibly know to whom you are referring. The *her* and the *she* you mention, it's rather vague."

"My betrothed," he snapped.

"I was not aware a married man could have one of those."

"You know very well I mean your sister," he growled.

"And I rightly do not know where you have scared her off to."

His eyes blazed with righteous indignation. "I did no such thing."

"Of course you did. Let there be no illusions between us. My sister ran away at the prospect of eating only one slice of toast in the morning." She ignored his arched brows. "Amongst other things."

"And these other things, they are all about love and happily ever after, yes?" he mocked.

She shrugged. "We Middletons *love* our breakfast."

"And you don't share your sister's view? That is why you married me?"

"I'm much more practical when it comes to matters of toast. But less so when it comes to starvation."

He scoffed. "Those rules are in place to ensure blooming health."

Blooming health? Who on earth was this man?

"It's *unhealthy* to change my diet from hearty breakfast to a meager slice of toast," Willow countered.

He sighed. A deep heavy exhale of breath. The hardness of his eyes, however, did not soften. "I will not argue the merits of my rules with you. However, it seems to me you are in need of a lesson as you have wittingly put your life in danger by slipping out last night. Do you have any idea how dangerous London is at night?"

In need of a lesson? From the stuffy Duke of St. Ives? Her temper exploded. *I think not*.

"I was perfectly safe last night and no, dear husband, it's not I in need of a lesson but you."

"And what lesson would that be?" he drawled.

"Respecting your wife's privacy," she declared. "From henceforth, you shall not set foot in my bedchambers without an invitation!"

Black eyes flashed.

Willow shut her mouth before she could take the words back. In hindsight, that might not have been the wisest declaration since her goal was to become with child. But then, she had no intention of accomplishing her goal on *his* terms—at least not as they were declared last night—and she refused to settle for less. Even if it meant putting her plan on hold for the time being.

"And what of your duties toward your husband?"

Willow brushed a wayward strand of hair from her face, suddenly pleased the reckless declaration had flown from her lips.

"What about them?"

A vein ticked in his jaw.

Willow shrugged. "You have made your point clear, as have I. I shall not neglect my duty to produce you an heir but neither shall I endure your huffing and puffing."

"I do not huff and puff!" Clearly offended, he dragged his hand through his hair.

"Once I have confirmed your seed has not taken root, I shall decide if I wish to endure another night of your . . ." she shot him A Look, "erratic breathing or not."

His eyes darkened, if that was at all possible. "You did more than endure, dear wife, you cried out in pleasure. And may I remind you, regular intercourse ensures a faster result," he pointed out. "And I can show you just how much you enjoyed it, again and again."

Heat pooled in her belly at the reminder. She wasn't about to let slip just how much last night had rocked her world. Not when he was still thinking to deny her that experience.

"Perhaps, but that was before you awakened me to the pleasures of the flesh and then threatened to deny me, most cruel of you. So if I am not to enjoy the siring of your heir, neither shall you."

His lips thinned.

Willow almost cracked a grin. She had the devil there. She meant it, too. Either he would change his rule or she would stick to hers. No small part of her hoped for the former.

"Besides, if your seed is as disciplined as you are," she said with the jut of her chin, "no further intercourse is required."

His eyes rolled over her in a sensual way, indicating he did not agree. She quickly quelled the sudden well of unbidden desire. Willow would not be intimidated or seduced by him. No matter that his low drawl stirred her senses to arousing life. She would maintain her composure.

"You don't mean that."

"I mean every word," Willow declared.

A wicked smile curved his lips "Is this your way of seducing me? Driving me wild with want?"

"Of course you would see it as such. No one has ever defied your wishes, have they?"

He glared down at her.

"If you wanted a biddable wife, Ambrose, you should not have set your sights on a Middleton. A wallflower might have been more to your taste for I am not a woman who wilts under a man's stern regard."

"In the battle of wills, Willow, you will lose."

Determination rose within her breast. "I suppose we shall see about that," she murmured.

From nowhere, he tossed the latest newspaper on the bed. Willow hadn't even realized he had it clutched in his hand. She drew the paper closer, reading the headline, printed in bold letters on the first page of the London Times.

The Duke of St. Ives marries the wrong Middleton.

Willow groaned. "That sounds about right," she muttered, reading on. Why had she harbored the faintest of hope that the scandal would not be splashed on the first page of the newspapers?

In what might be considered the greatest deception in London's aristocracy, one of the most powerful men in England was duped in a grand heathen wedding swap.

Well, Willow mused, it could hardly be a wedding swap if one of the parties walked away without a husband.

Though the duke seemed taken with his bride—even kissed her most ardently before the priest!—one has to wonder whether the Dowager's fainting spell was due to her failing health or bearing witness to the stain of black taint spreading across her coveted family name.

Willow flinched.

"I see you agree with my sentiments," the duke snatched the paper from her fingers. "It's a rare pleasure to read the paper and see they refer to my wife as a heathen."

"There are worse words to be referred as." Like strumpet. Or harridan. Or fishwife. "They are just speculating. Speculation is good."

"And how is that, my little heathen wife?"

Willow sighed, her eyes lifting to meet the hard onyx crystals of the duke's.

"Speculation can be controlled. It can be spun in any way you choose, so you can stop glaring at me and attempt to salvage your mother's antics. Had she not sobbed like a child and fainted, most of these rumors might have been avoided."

"I've taken steps to resolve this mess."

He had? "What steps?"

He shrugged. "Dashwood and I are collaborating stories that the name of my bride got mixed up with her sister's."

"But you courted Holly, not me."

"I say, and Dashwood says, I courted you."

Willow rolled her eyes. "Are you going to punish me for slipping out?"

"I am not a beast. But I do have boundaries and you have crossed them all." He paused, his eyes meeting hers. "However, since we do not know one another all that well, a certain leeway is to be allowed."

Willow blinked up at him in shock. He did not wait for a reply but pivoted on his heel and strode from the room.

"Read the damn rules," he snapped over his shoulder. "Because if you ever put yourself in danger again, I will lock you in your damn chamber for a year."

She did not doubt that he would do it, too.

Willow fell back on the bed with a sigh. This was not how she expected her morning to begin. Neither had she expected such a relatively mild response from her husband. He must have been furious in discovering her gone. And then there was the headline of today's paper. She'd fully expected some form of punishment from him. As a matter of fact, she had rather thought he'd transform into an ogre.

But he hadn't.

This was not the character of a man everyone believed to be a tyrant.

If you ever put yourself in danger again…

In danger. Interesting choice of words. Not if Willow ever defied his rules, but if she ever put herself in danger again. Indeed, perhaps something else was at hand here. She'd have to give the matter some lengthy thought.

She was still not reading those damn rules.

Chapter 9

A Duchess ought not to snort at her husband.

That should be in her husband's little pamphlet of rules, if it wasn't already, for it was likely to become a daily habit of hers to snort at his buffoonery. And Willow doubted he'd approve of that.

In fact, it probably was in there, but she still refused to read the infuriating stack of paper. Instead, she dressed and headed down to breakfast.

On entering the breakfast room, it was clear that the battle lines had been drawn long before Willow had woken to an irate husband. Indeed, they'd likely been drawn before the wedding breakfast, if she had to guess.

Not a single spread had been laid out. There was no evidence that the duke or the dowager had ever been present in the room at all. Instead, only one, lonely little plate had been set.

On that plate was an even lonelier slice of toast.

Her scowl deepened.

He claimed he wasn't a beast.

Willow snorted. Evidence proved otherwise.

Apart from this absurdity, the sad sight of an empty dining room was not something Willow was used to. In their home, breakfast was a lively affair. Any meal, in truth, was a cheerful event. Even tea times were spent together as a family. It was across the table where stories were shared and events recounted.

Willow swept the cold room with a speculative glance. Not even the opulence of the space was enough to bring it a measure of warmth. No candles decorated the surface of the table to suggest evening meals by candlelight. No forgotten ribbon or glove littered the table. No laughter or stories echoed off the walls. It was a hollow space, bereft of even the simplest form of intimate decoration.

It was the saddest thing Willow had ever come across.

And it wasn't just the dining room. There was no cheerfulness in her new home, she realized. The whole house hadn't contained laughter in a long while.

She turned to the footman standing in the corner, unmoving as a statue. "Where is the breakfast?" she asked, wanting verbal confirmation from someone other than her husband that there was no breakfast in the house at all.

"No breakfast has been prepared, Your Grace."

"Then what am I to eat?" Willow pointed to the table. "A slice of cold hard toast?"

The footman cleared his throat, uncomfortable.

Willow glared at the toast. That slice represented the war with her husband. Her sadness turned to anger.

This was ridiculous. She could probably live off a slice of bread in the morning but what was the point of being a duchess if she could not eat like a duchess? They could at least have added some tea to swallow the slice down.

It occurred to Willow this was why Ambrose hadn't locked her in her room or raved on about how she'd slipped out in the dead of night. He'd already planned due reward. The duke's reprisal wasn't loud or obvious. No indeed, his tactics were far subtler than that. He would mete out his displeasure with her in the form of cold, dry toast.

Just like her husband's black little heart.

"There's not even a dash of butter," she muttered.

"'Twas his lordship's orders, Your Grace."

Willow shot the footman a scathing look. She already knew that. The poor man looked ready to bolt through the door in response. She sighed. It wasn't the footman's fault that her husband was a browbeating beast. But she also knew that the servant would report her reaction to her husband as soon as she left the room.

If she wasn't so hungry, which only succeeded in fueling her annoyance, she might have laughed. She'd give the man something to report then. It was high time some change came into her husband's life. A rude awakening, if you will.

It was also time to make allies in this enemy territory. And her first ally clearly ought to be the cook. One did not fight battles on an empty belly.

"What is your name?" she asked the footman, her arms crossing over her chest.

"Wendell, Your Grace."

"Well, Wendell, I am the lady of the house, am I not?" she asked him, this time infusing a softer tone into her voice.

"Yes, Your Grace."

"Which means I am in charge of running this household, correct?"

"Yes, Your Grace."

"That includes the menu, does it not?"

The footman paused, clearing his throat.

Willow arched a brow.

"Yes, Your Grace," he murmured, shifting on his feet. "That is how things are usually run."

Usually. Meaning not here.

Too bad, Willow thought. That, too, was about to change.

"Well, Wendell, it appears you have a choice to make."

"Your Grace?"

"You can continue to follow the duke's instructions, in which case I will consider you my enemy, or you can come over to the right side of it, and I shall consider you my friend. Of course, you will not lose your job, as I, the lady of the house, am also in charge of hiring servants and letting them go."

The footman swallowed.

"You will not be relieved of your position if you choose my husband's side, of course," Willow reassured. She did not wish to make allies based on threats. "I'd understand if you did for reasons of loyalty and so forth, though I would kindly ask you to leave the room so as not to impede my next plan of action."

He looked surprised by her words and Willow thought she saw a flash of admiration. She needed the servants on her side. It would show her husband she carried some weight.

"A change will be a good thing, Your Grace," Wendell said after a brief moment of pause and Willow flashed him a blinding smile.

"My thoughts exactly. Now tell me, what other instructions has my husband handed out?"

"Your Grace is to be escorted at all times."

"Even in the house?"

Wendell nodded. "I am to shadow your every move."

Willow scowled. Last night, to her relief, when she had returned home, she had found no footman stationed outside her door. Poppy must not have heard correctly. Or the duke had changed his mind. Needless to say, she'd be watched from today.

"Are you to lurk outside my chambers at night, too?"

Wendell flushed. "That would be Thomas, Your Grace."

"I see. And I take it you are to report my every step to the duke?"

Wendell nodded.

Willow had not underestimated her husband, he was a man with pride after all, but this seemed way beyond the pale. Hopefully, now that Wendell was on her side, she would not feel so alone in this cold house while she delved deeper towards the root of her husband's need for control.

"Where is the dowager?" Willow asked.

"She retired to Bath this morning, Your Grace."

Willow blinked in surprise. *She had*? Not that Willow was complaining, but she hadn't expected her mother-in-law to leave at all.

"Did the duke send her away or did she decide to go on her own?"

"I believe the duke had a hand in the departure, Your Grace."

So Ambrose had sent his mother away. She recalled how he said he'd begun to resolve matters. Sending the Dragon Duchess away must be part of his plan.

And with the dowager gone, they might just accomplish something.

"That is good," Willow murmured, sparing another look of disgust at the toast. She was so ravenous, she felt tempted to snatch it up just to stave off her hunger. But she decided if she were to prove a point, the toast should remain lifeless on that plate.

Her belly protested as she turned away.

"Wendell, if you will lead me to the kitchen, I would like a word with the cook. And please inform my husband that the toast was left uneaten." Let him believe she was starving.

"Of course, Your Grace."

The cook, much to Willow's enjoyment, was adorable. A plump woman with kind eyes, she had been rightly shocked when Willow appeared in her kitchen. But after a few words of encouragement and the prospect of a better atmosphere, Cook was on her side as well.

They both agreed the time had come to liven up the dining room once more. And what better way to erase the gloom-ridden energy the breakfast of blazing stares had left behind than coming up with a menu fit for a king and queen?

"I suppose the duke will be quite put out with me tonight," Willow said, taking a bite of buttered toast spread with raspberry jam and cream. She planned to dine tonight. With or without him.

"I suspect he will," Wendell said, swallowing the last of his coffee.

Cook nodded. "It's about time the dining room is put to good use again. It has been far too long since we heard laughter echoing off these walls."

Willow nodded, understanding from Cook that Ambrose hadn't always been this way. This made her more resolved to draw out the man beneath the mask. And more hopeful that their marriage could have a kinder, less warring future.

"Have you been with the family long?" she asked Cook.

"Since before the lad's birth."

"Then you know why the duke changed?"

Wendell suddenly looked uncomfortable. "That is also not our place to say." He shot Cook a warning look.

"Oh posh, it's high time for some change to come about this place." Cook glanced at Willow with sad eyes. "If it helps your cause, child, you must know that His Grace was never the same after his sister, Lady Celia, passed away."

He'd lost a sister? How had she not known? "How did Lady Celia die?"

"An ailment of the heart, the doctor claimed," Cook answered.

How sad, Willow thought as her chest tightened. She could not imagine losing any one of her sisters. "How long ago was this?"

"Ten years," Wendell said.

Ten years! It seemed an insurmountable amount of time. Enough time for any one's ways to become engraved in stone. "Let us hope I can find a way to win the duke over," Willow murmured. *And find a way to heal him.* "And my mother-in-law," she muttered as an afterthought.

"Do not worry too much over her, dearie. As soon as you win the Duke, the Dowager will follow suit," Cook said.

"That will be hard to do with her crying about the disgrace and shame I brought to the family," Willow said, sipping on her tea.

"Oh, she will come around, you just wait and see, dear."

"Let us hope that is true."

A part of Willow still wondered if her husband had more motives for sending his mother away—like say, to clear the battlefield. A brazen assumption, yes, but not one she'd put past her husband. He was, after all, a master puppeteer, pulling the strings of people in a most clever, if not unscrupulous, way.

This knowledge that he was once a carefree man made the situation so much more bittersweet. Her heart practically bled that he may still be deeply hurt by the loss of his sister. It changed everything.

Well, almost everything.

Willow recognized the flutters in her stomach with some alarm. Interest. Curiosity. It sparked to life. She *wanted* to discover that man—the carefree man with the impassioned heart.

"If it hadn't been for the late duke's will. . ." Cook was saying.

"What?" Willow's eyes snapped back to the woman. "What about the late duke's will?

"It is rumored there was a clause in the will."

Wendell groaned. Willow and Cook both ignored him.

"A clause?" Willow asked, intrigued. "What type of clause?"

Cook leaned forward, lowering her voice. It was positively gratifying. "A clause that commanded the duke to wed within twelve months of his father's death."

"Or what?" Willow asked, curious as to how a man with so much power could be commanded to wed.

"Or the duke would forfeit his *entire* inheritance."

"*No*," Willow said, shaking her head.

"*Yes*," Cook said, both she and Wendell nodding now.

Dear lord.

It explained so much. Why he married in haste. His dubious methods in doing so. His clear distaste for the marriage. How would it feel to have one's entire world placed in jeopardy by a dead relative? To have no choice on the timing of such a significant matter as marriage? All while he was seemingly still grieving a sister. And, Willow assumed, the clause aside, a father.

The Perks Of Being A Duchess

She, at least, had entered the marriage of her own free will. It'd been a drastic and somewhat crazed decision, but it'd been her decision nonetheless. No one had forced her.

Willow made a decision there and then. Ambrose might not know this yet, but Willow intended to restore brightness to his life. She had a feeling that a little light in his world might go a long way towards bringing back the man he once was—the man she'd like to become acquainted with.

Filled with renewed determination, she turned to her new allies. "About tonight. . ."

Chapter 10

"My wife has declared war, Benson," Ambrose told his valet, who had been with him for the past twelve years. The man had never been afraid to voice his opinion, and over the years, Ambrose had come to value it.

"War, Your Grace?"

"Would you perhaps have a better word for what has transpired in this house?"

And perhaps the term war *was* a bit overdramatic, but it certainly felt like he had marched straight into a battlefield.

For Christ's sake, he had expected that when he set eyes on her this morning, all the pent-up anger over the wedding and his fury over her midnight rendezvous would tumble forth in an avalanche of rage.

But had that happened?

No. Instead, she had bloody floored him with her big, blue, innocent eyes and her rumpled hair. Most of his anger had fled at the sight of her beneath the crumpled sheets and was replaced by hot burning desire. The temptation to take her into his arms right then and there had been so great, his heart had nearly exploded from his chest.

The marriage was not going the way he had thought at all.

It was damned disturbing.

"She is new to your ways, Your Grace," Benson agreed. "But I have every confidence in your lordship's ability to court the duchess."

Court? If Ambrose had ever learned to splutter, he'd be doing that now. "I have no reason to court my wife, Benson, hence the word wife."

"It is my understanding, Your Grace, that all women wish to be courted, one way or another."

"And it is my understanding that wives ought to do wifely things and not act out," Ambrose muttered.

Why the hell had this happened to him? He should never have given Holly those rules before their wedding. But he had foolishly suffered a moment of guilt and had not wanted her to wed him without knowing who she was marrying. If only he had held his conscience in check for a few more days.

He thought he'd be gaining a wife that would be easy to protect, easy to ensure her health and safety. Instead, he'd gotten one that would fight him at every step he took to enforce that protection. Willow was strong, resistant, and, though Ambrose hadn't thought it possible, just as stubborn as he.

More disturbing even, as he had looked down on her sleeping, waiting for her to awaken, he recalled every soft sigh she'd given at his touch, and a single question had popped into his mind: *Did he even want to master his wife?*

All he could damn well think about was whether forcing his rules on her would make her touches become less eager. Would her soft moans disappear altogether? Would she still respond to him with unbridled passion or would the fire in her eyes die along with her freedom of spirit?

The answer had set his heart leaping in his chest.

What the devil was wrong with him? He never reacted this way. He never second-guessed himself.

Control meant safety.

Safety meant life.

Safety meant never feeling that loss again.

Then why did he fear a different kind of loss if he succeeded? Why did he feel so conflicted?

Because Celia might still be alive had she taken care of her health.

"It ought to be easy enough," his valet was saying, tugging at his jacket, "to win the duchess over."

"Win over my wife? Have you not heard a word I said? She has declared war. Battle lines have been drawn."

"And how does a man win a battle with one's wife," Benson ventured, "if not by winning her over?"

"My wife is rebelling against me, Benson. She believes me a tyrant," Ambrose pressed on. "Winning her over with hearts and roses is out of the question."

"No need to trouble Your Grace with hearts and roses. Just let the duchess see your lordship in a different light. A softer one, perhaps. Less tyrannical." He gave Ambrose a once over. "Though that may take some work."

"What the hell does that mean?"

"Be nice to your wife, Your Grace, *listen* to her wishes. Take her to the theatre."

"Let me tell you something, Benson. Women are like bloodhounds. Once they sense any form of weakness, they'll go straight for your throat. If I suddenly court my wife, she will smell blood in the water."

And what did Benson know about being nice, anyway? Most of the time the man was as sour as an old bottle of wine. Besides, Willow knew she was not his chosen bride. She'd smell the insincerity of the action.

Therefore, he could not be *nice* to his wife.

Ten curses upon his father's soul! He'd never be in this mess if it weren't for his old man's machinations.

There had been a moment, after he'd done everything in his power to contest the will, where he decided to hell with it, he did not need any of the unentailed land. He would restore the family coffers on his own.

But his father had been a clever bastard.

While Ambrose did not mind losing all that wealth and lands, he still had to think of his mother and brother. And in the event that Ambrose failed to marry, all that lands and wealth would be donated to a distant relative Ambrose had never even heard about. Meaning he'd have no funds to support his family. Meaning they'd suffer as he worked to build his wealth back up.

Ambrose would never allow that.

Yes, his father had been a clever bastard.

"Damn my father and his rotten hide," he muttered, his words imbued with bitterness.

"The late duke meant well," Benson said, though his words lacked conviction.

"You are still hanging on to that fairytale, Benson? The bastard meant to control me from his bloody grave."

The irony wasn't lost on him. He, Ambrose Brandon Jonathan Griffin, who sought to control all things, was controlled by a ghost.

"He controls you no longer, Your Grace. The requirement of the will was met. The late duke has no hold over you anymore."

"But he won. He got what he wanted."

"He only wins if you are miserable for the rest of your life, Your Grace. Your resentment towards him is what's keeping his hold," Benson reasoned. "Let go of that, find happiness and you win."

"Only you would think that makes a wit of sense," Ambrose muttered. Unfortunately, he suspected his valet might be right. His father hadn't taken well to his announcement that Ambrose, his heir, planned to remain unwed and let the title pass on to the spare. Because the spare had no spare. And according to his father, he hadn't spent Ambrose's entire life preparing him for the ducal responsibilities just so he could toss it aside.

Their relationship had been strained ever since.

And since he'd caved to his father's dictate, he'd been deserted at the altar, married the wrong woman, and was now at war with his wife.

"Your Grace has already taken the first step, even if your lordship doesn't realize it yet."

"And how is that?"

"You sent your mother to retire to the warm waters of Bath."

"That hardly signifies anything, except to alleviate the strain on my nerves."

"If Your Grace says so," his valet murmured, a smile curving his lips.

"I do say so," Ambrose growled, glaring at the man.

Impetuous valet. And damn outspoken. And an utter nuisance. Because now Ambrose was calling into question the reason he sent his mother away. *No*, Ambrose told himself. He was not. He sent his mother away to give them all the chance to adjust and for the dust to settle on any scandal.

"Then perhaps I may offer some advice, Your Grace?"

"Don't let me hold you back." Ambrose gnashed his teeth. "You never do."

"Reconsider wooing the duchess."

"Out of the question," Ambrose pronounced. Then, after a small pause, "Why the hell would I do that? More importantly, what would it accomplish?"

"To keep the peace, Your Grace." Benson smoothed out Ambrose's coat. "A woman in love is a woman without willfulness."

Or more of it, Ambrose thought darkly. Look where that had gotten him with Holly Middleton. She'd fancied herself in love with him and abandoned him the moment she realized the feeling wasn't mutual.

As if reading his thoughts, Benson said, "It seems to me, Your Grace, that the duchess does not hold the same romantic ideals as your former betrothed. There is no risk. She is already your wife."

Ambrose grunted.

That was true, but the last thing he wanted was for his wife to pester him to change his ways because he had wooed her. Or God forbid, expect him to return her doe-eyed stares because she believed him to hold affection for her.

But, his valet had made a valid point. If his wife held some—even a little—form of affection for him . . . wouldn't that make the situation a bit easier?

She could not leave him—she was his wife. She might be suspicious or believe him insincere, but that was about the worst of it. And Willow did not strike him as the type to abandon anyone.

She valued family.

And he was part of that family now.

He tested the thought in his mind.

Woo his wife. Win her over.

Ambrose was still not convinced that meant a whole lot. Willow refused to read his rules, had snuck out of their home, and God only knows what else. And given the choice, she would choose her sisters over him, he was sure of it.

But what to do then? It was way beyond the bounds of his experience. Was wooing her truly the answer? Winning her over? He was at a total loss. The need to control simmered beneath his skin. But there was something new—another desire altogether was forming. It felt suspiciously like the desire to *please* his wife.

Absolutely, completely and utterly absurd.

No, courting his wife, Ambrose decided, was out of the question. He enjoyed her company too much already. More time spent in her presence would be dangerous. A marriage of convenience was the best option for them both. As he had intended.

"The duchess," he told his valet, "will soon enough learn her place. I will not be managed. All it will take is to find the right incentive."

"Incentive, Your Grace?"

"Reduce her pin money, for one."

Forbid her to see her family for another.

It would be the ultimate inducement, Ambrose supposed. One he wasn't certain he wished to enforce.

"There is always seduction, Your Grace."

Ambrose shot his valet an aggrieved look. The man would not give up.

Seduction, he supposed, formed part of the convenience in marriage of convenience.

There was only one problem.

Ambrose had made a brash declaration to withhold pleasure, because he'd felt something very akin to *emotion*. And he simply could not go back on his word now. Not after he'd been so arrogantly cocksure of himself.

A frown puckered his brow.

He glanced at Benson, who suspiciously resembled a man trying his best to suppress a grin.

"I'm still your employer," Ambrose snapped out.

"Of course, Your Grace." He handed Ambrose his gloves. "But if I may point out, your only confidante is your valet."

"Not so. I confide in my brother, as well."

"When Lord Jonathan is present, yes."

"Your point?" Ambrose saw nothing wrong with that. Most gentlemen were tedious in any case. Benson at least added some impertinent spice to his life. And he was meeting his brother at White's in a few hours.

"Change is an uncomfortable occurrence," Benson shrugged. "It is also necessary. And perhaps it is time to make a new *friend*."

"You mean my wife?" Ambrose said dryly. "Do you ever give up?"

Benson appeared unperturbed. "It is important to note that even though Your Grace does not deal well with change, without change, England would not be the formidable country it is today."

What the bloody hell was Benson getting at?

He was formidable enough.

He was also happy for his life to remain forever unchanged. But that was no longer possible. Change was happening whether he liked it or not.

"I only mean to say that oftentimes we make life harder than it needs to be."

"Spoken like a true philosopher." Ambrose raised an artful brow. "Any advice on how to silence an impertinent valet?"

"Perhaps a gold signet ring is in order?" Benson suggested, and Ambrose laughed.

If only he could snuff out all the enchanting thoughts of his wife that stubbornly clung to his brain.

One piece of good fortune was his mother, who had been overjoyed to retire to Bath. Ambrose had expected more tears. Instead, he'd been greeted with a rare smile.

Ambrose would never understand women.

Shrugging on his gloves and accepting the hat from Benson, Ambrose wondered whether there was more to the primal urge he had to claim his wife in every possible way. And since Ambrose was not a man to wallow in denial, he wondered whether he would arrive at the end of this battle unscathed and unchanged.

He bloody hoped so.

Chapter 11

Ambrose was dreaming. That was the only explanation for finding a hundred lit candles glowing in his dining room. That was his first clue that it must be a dream—he did not even own *that* many candles. And even if he did, he'd never light them all at once. It was a hazard—a fire begging to burst out. The second clue was the presence of his glowing wife—a sparkling diamond—who was covered in a deep plum gown of velvet silk and standing in the center of the room. She exhumed radiance. A picture of grace. A goddess bathed in brilliance. Ambrose could not tear his gaze away.

A dream, certainly.

"Ambrose," she greeted him with a smile. "You are just in time. I was about to retire."

He physically jolted at the sound of her sultry voice, which plunged him into reality. This wasn't a dream. It was really bloody happening.

"In time for . . ." Ambrose hedged.

"Port."

His gaze flicked to the table that had been set for two. One plate remained untouched. "I usually take dinner at the club."

She nodded. "So I gathered, but nevertheless, you are in time for a glass of dessert."

He crooked a brow, his eyes darting to all the candles again.

"The room lacked warmth," she said as if reading his mind. But she could not possibly know what he was thinking. Because he was thinking of all the different ways the house could go up in flames.

Along with all the ways he might erupt into flames as well.

"Was it necessary to light a hundred candles?" Ambrose muttered, his brows snapping together. "Two or three candles would have sufficed."

"It's not *that* many," she said, her gaze sweeping the room with delight. "It's rather homely, do you not agree?"

No. Not homely. Dangerous. And if they did not accidently set the house on fire, then maybe he could enjoy the ambiance. Maybe. But not having the heart to erase her smile, he said, or rather grumbled, "I suppose."

"Shall we . . ." she trailed off as her gaze drifted to a point beyond him.

Ambrose groaned.

"It's blazing cold tonight," his brother said, shouldering past him, shaking off his coat. Jonathan came up short when he spotted Willow. "Well, what do we have here?" Then his mouth spread into a wolfish grin. "You must be the lovely, famed duchess I've heard so much about."

Ambrose had forgotten about his brother.

"You must have another duchess in mind," Willow said, walking over to the nearby table to pour them each a glass of port. "I'm certainly not famed."

"Then there's another Duchess of St. Ives?" He sent Ambrose an amused look. "I'm not sure that's legal, brother."

Willow whipped around. "Wait, *you're* Lord Jonathan?"

"The resemblance is uncanny, right?"

"Not even a little bit."

He accepted the glass of port from Willow and Ambrose did the same.

Jonathan cocked his head then, swirling the glass in his hand. "Though I imagine I bear little resemblance to your imaginings of me, generally speaking."

"Imaginings?"

"Yes, the ones with horns and a tail."

"And why would I imagine that?"

Jonathan shrugged. "I missed your wedding. Surely, I am a devil for that. I thought that would elicit some angry imaginings, at least."

Willow smiled. "If you must know, I imagined you with crooked fangs, actually."

He laughed, flashing them a peek at straight white teeth. "I will take that over horns any day."

"Forgive me, Lord Jonathan, but I thought you were on tour? Have you returned recently?"

"If you mean a tour of all the best—"

"Jonathan," Ambrose growled, and his brother laughed.

"Never mind," Jonathan said, casting a quick glance at him before returning his attention to Willow. "Though I must admit, I was intrigued to hear the details of my brother's wedding. A few interesting events to note, certainly."

"Really? I thought very little of it would come as a surprise, given your father's will. Surely such a situation breeds of chaos."

"I—" Jonathan began to reply, but Ambrose cut him off.

"You know about the clause," Ambrose demanded, staring at his wife.

"Yes," she answered. "I've heard all about your father's will. I must admit, it was quite a shocking discovery."

Ambrose felt the blood leave his body. But for his mother, brother, and solicitor, no one was ever supposed to know about that. It was damned embarrassing. "Who told you?"

"It hardly matters where I heard it, only that I did," she glanced at him sideways. "It does explain some of your surly moods. Not to mention your methods in courting my sister."

Jonathan laughed, plopping himself down in a chair. "She is a resourceful one, brother, I am pleased to discover."

"That she is," Ambrose muttered, sweeping the room with a glance. "It appears she even has the servants wrapped around her finger."

Willow turned to him, her eyes startlingly blue, even in the candlelight. "So it's true, then? You married because of a clause in your father's will?"

What else could he do but nod? The truth was out, there was nothing to do but move on.

"Why, then, did you wait so long to secure a wife?" she asked. "It seemed like something you ought to have done sooner."

"My brother did his damndest to find a loophole," Jonathan interrupted before Ambrose could speak. "But as you are well aware, he failed."

Ambrose sent his brother a stony look, and when he spoke, there was an edge of impatience to his voice. "Thank you for pointing out my failure."

"A pleasure." Jonathan winked at Willow. "Except I would not call securing such a lovely wife a failure."

"I think it's about time you leave," Ambrose all but growled at his brother, who remained stubbornly seated on his arse.

"Wait a minute," his wife spoke up, puzzled. Ambrose grimaced at the open curiosity in her voice. "Why did your father put such a clause in his will? It seems a bit cruel."

"It bloody well was," Ambrose growled.

At that, his wife narrowed her eyes on him. "What did you do?"

"What makes you assume I did anything?" He demanded, offended.

"The clause," she said meeting his gaze. "You must have done something for your father to add such a thing."

Right.

"Oh, he did," Jonathan piped up from where he sat.

Ambrose shot him a glare.

"Well?" she pressed. "Are you going to tell me or not?"

Ambrose lifted his eyes to hers and sighed. She already knew about the clause, might as well reveal the part that prompted it. "I announced to my father I would never marry. He did not take it well."

"Of course not, you were his heir."

Ambrose nodded. "Yes, I was, but Jonathan could marry and supply the necessary heirs. However, my father objected."

"Fiercely," Jonathan agreed.

Ambrose cut his brother a look, before turning back to his wife. "Yes. My father claimed he hadn't groomed me my entire life just for me to waste my birthright."

"Let's not forget the argument about how *I* was the spare, and how I could not be relied upon to provide offspring before perishing, given my lifestyle, and no heirs to the St. Ives line meant the entire world would be doomed," Jonathan joined in. "It was all very riveting."

"There was that," Ambrose agreed. Which, all things considered, had been a valid point. But after Celia's death, he had wanted nothing to do with anything that could cost him his heart, so he had stood firm against his father.

"But why the aversion to marriage?" Willow asked. "You are a duke, providing an heir is one of your many duties."

Ambrose hesitated. His aversion was based on his fear of losing another loved one—he'd never been in denial about that. But while his family, all except his father, had understood that, explaining it to his wife was altogether different, and he wasn't sure this was the moment to do it—especially with Jonathan present to comment.

"There is no need to explain," Willow suddenly said. Her soft whisper smoothed over him like an excellent year of cognac. "I think I understand."

"You do?" Both him and Jonathan blurted at the same time.

"Your family suffered a painful loss when you lost your sister."

Christ, how had she learned about Celia?

He supposed if she learned about the will, then learning about Celia wasn't that much of a surprise. Her death was public knowledge, after all. Still, it somehow hurt to hear the truth of that statement in her voice.

"I'm truly sorry such a tragedy befell your family," she continued further. "I'm sure your father just wished to secure your family's bloodline beyond the benefit of a doubt. You all dealt with the loss in different ways."

Ambrose couldn't answer, his heart in his throat.

"Well, I for one don't think my brother married the wrong woman after all," Jonathan said sipping his port. There was a roughness to his voice that hadn't been there before.

"The wrong woman married me after the other one ran away," Ambrose pointed out, drawing the topic away from the intensity that poured into the room.

He'd thought his wife long since retired when he entered his home after supper at the club. Had he known she'd still be up, he'd have sent his brother home. The last thing he wanted was for them to conspire behind his back. Or bond right before his eyes—like they were doing now.

"Yes, yes, and you are not a man that will let such a slight go, as evident from me being married off in revenge. You should work on your people skills, brother."

Ambrose felt his jaw tighten.

"You will do your brother's bidding, then?" Willow asked Jonathan, her eyes alight with interest.

"The answer to that, my dear," Jonathan slanted a smile her way, "will depend on whether my brother is in the room with me or not."

His wife laughed like it was the funniest bloody thing in the world. To Ambrose's amazement, she did not press the issue. Instead, she smiled sweetly and asked, "Why, pray tell, did you not attend the wedding, Lord Jonathan?"

Ambrose turned to his brother and cocked a brow. "Yes, Jonathan, why did you not attend our wedding?"

"Ah, well, in an unfortunate set of circumstance, I was indisposed," Jonathan said, a slight flush coloring his features.

Ambrose snorted, drawing their attention to him. He said nothing, only lifted his glass to sip on his port, waiting to see what his wife had to say. But she just arched a brow right back at him, taking a sip of *her* port.

Ambrose felt his teeth grinding.

It was going to be a long night.

An hour later, Willow watched her brother-in-law bid his farewell, quite uncertain what to make of him. He looked nothing like her husband. His hair was a shade or two darker, his eyes a light brandy color, not as dark and intense as Ambrose's. And his nose was slightly more crooked, as though it had once been broken.

By all accounts, he ought to be in possession of horns, and deformed teeth, for all the images she had conjured in her mind after learning Ambrose wished to wed him to Holly. He was supposed to be the enemy.

But he seemed carefree and charming to her. And he placed a rather improper kiss on her wrist, drawing a scowl from her husband.

"My brother must have done something right, to wed such a lovely creature as you." His words were insanely flattering, and Willow found herself grinning up at him.

"That's enough," Ambrose snapped. "Stop flirting with my wife."

Willow suppressed a grin and Lord Jonathan took his leave with a shallow bow. She had wanted to ask him so many things, but had refrained from putting both men on the spot. She aimed to build bridges, not burn them. And they had only been married two days. If she was to succeed in changing Ambrose's mind about Holly, they had to become better acquainted with one another. And tonight, short interaction though it was, had been a start.

Plus, she had met Lord Jonathan and he was not the ogre she had conjured in her mind's eye. He was a man she could appeal to, if nothing else.

But even beyond the brothers' appearances, their hearts were also as different as dawn and dusk. And if there was one thing Willow had learned of her husband tonight, it was that the seed of all his actions came from his heart—whether that action was misguided or not.

Willow turned to her husband. "I think I shall retire as well."

"Permit me to escort you to your chamber," he murmured and began leading her to the hallway that would take them to the staircase. "You should have sent word about dinner. Had I known, I'd have joined you."

"I left a note on your desk, but it seems you were out all day," Willow murmured with a sidelong glance at him.

"I met Jonathan at the club."

"Ah." They reached the top of the landing.

"You do look beautiful tonight," he said suddenly, peering down at her. His voice had a sinful rasp to it. His eyes . . . they had taken on a new intensity, especially when they lowered and focused on her lips.

"Are you saying that to soften me or do you mean it?" Willow asked, unable to help herself. She didn't know how much of a game—or a war—this was to her husband. And part of her wanted the words to be real.

He raised his eyes to meet her own, his green gaze steady. "I would never say those words if I did not mean them."

Oh.

"Am I still barred from your chamber?"

The question was sudden and yet expected given the heat between them. It brought along with it all sorts of provocative feelings. Feelings that demanded to be explored. Willow paid them no mind. She was stronger than her wanton longings.

"Beyond a doubt," she breathed.

"Not even a sliver of a doubt?"

"Ambrose . . ."

He leaned into her until her back was firmly pressed into the door, an arm reaching out on either side of her face, caging her in.

Her breathing accelerated. The more she tried to shove her thoughts—her wicked, wicked thoughts—in a box and shut the lid tight, the fiercer they grew in their strength.

Then his mouth was slanting across hers, and Willow did not possess the power to push him away. Leisurely, with infinite sensuality, he kissed her, his tongue coaxing her mouth apart. It felt like more than a kiss. It felt like an enticement. Like a whispered secret. Like seduction. And beneath the tenderness of his lips, she felt the urgency. The desire. His. Hers.

Mine.

Panic flooded her at the sentiment. She tore her hands off his chest and fumbled for the doorknob behind her. She broke the kiss.

"Will—"

She turned and escaped into her room, slamming the door shut before Ambrose could finish her name. She fell back against door inside her room, breathing hard.

Well, that certainly hadn't gone as planned.

Chapter 12

She following evening found them dancing at the Cleveland ball. One moment, Willow had admired a particularly obnoxious shade of yellow breeches and the next, the cords of the first waltz that evening had struck up. Ambrose had turned to her, his dark eyes alight with sincerity, and asked her to dance. At first, Willow had been stunned—no words escaped her lips. Her composure, thank God, had recovered quite quickly.

She was in his arms.

His strong, muscular, powerful arms. Surrounded by the woody musk of his scent. Why that thrilled her so much was not up for debate. They were at odds with each other. Or at least Willow thought they were. Last night had sent her mind spiraling. Ambrose had kissed her. Honestly, he mussed up her brain. And Lord Jonathan was *here*, in London. Always had been.

What Willow did know was that she was not supposed to feel this delighted at the prospect of dancing with her husband.

For the life of her, she could not determine the angle he was playing at. But then again, a waltz was hardly the stuff of war. A kiss was more debatable. Except in both cases, his proximity and overwhelming presence bestowed chaos on her senses.

Or was that, perhaps, his plan?

Regardless, he was an excellent dancer. So good, in fact, that with every step he took, her body burned with greater desire to draw nearer to him still. Which made him exceptional in two things so far—dancing and . . . well, three things then, Willow mused, if she counted lovemaking, which she indeed did, and kissing. The thought made her eyes drift to his lips.

How can I be so obsessed with a mouth?

And thinking about his lips caused her mind to wander over to their first night. And she *so* did not want to wonder about that in the middle of a ballroom.

But how could she not think about that, with his body so sensually guiding hers in their dance? Willow felt a hot flush spread across her neck and ears.

For goodness's sake!

She had to get a hold of herself. But really, was there anything this man did not excel at?

Oh yes. Yes, there was. Namely relationships.

And communication. But she wasn't inclined to dwell on that at the moment, not while dancing in his arms.

For this moment, however fleeting, she could close her eyes and make-believe. They were in love. They were happy. Her husband was not a stick-in-the-mud duke with control issues, and she was not a woman who had married a man to use him as a stallion.

This night, this moment, almost seemed like a small reprieve.

It was also their first night out in public, and all eyes were on them, watching, observing, and waiting for the faintest mistake on their part.

Any other time, Willow would have danced herself dizzy or aided her cousin Belle in some mischief. But tonight, she had entered the marble halls of the ballroom at her husband's side, head held high.

Not once had he left her side, introducing her to various acquaintances. Everyone clamored to get a peek at the couple of the season. They were like wolves, waiting for the first sign of weakness.

Let them watch, Willow thought. No matter what happened between her and Ambrose, she would not give cause for the gossipmongers to spread their ill will.

So she savored the sensation of being twirled around and around, and with every turn, it seemed like his hand on her back slid lower. Or was that her imagination? She glanced up at him to see his eyes glowing as they stared down at her.

Willow wondered if this would be their only dance tonight. She did not imagine that a lesser dance—the quadrille, for example—would tempt a man such as Ambrose. He was much too contained for that.

A wild thought suddenly occurred to her. Was she allowed to dance with other gentlemen?

She scrunched up her brow.

Since she refused to read the rules, she wasn't sure. But then, she excelled at breaking rules—'twas her skill. Of course, instinct told her he wouldn't mind as long as she remained above reproach.

Willow kept her gaze locked on the duke in an attempt to decipher his mood. Which was impossible. He had been acting strangely all evening, though she couldn't quite put her finger on exactly how or what it might be.

As usual, his posture was stiff and uncompromising. But at the same time, he appeared *less* so. Was this his way of putting on a false air that nothing was amiss?

"You are an excellent dancer," Willow murmured on another whirl.

"I do not dance often," he returned.

"I would not have guessed from your skill."

This close to him, Willow found herself fascinated by the stubble on his cheeks. He hadn't seemed to have shaved since the wedding—so unlike him, she thought.

For some unfathomable reason the rough coat struck her as significant, but Willow did not know why it would.

"Do you not enjoy dancing?" she asked. The grip on her hand tightened.

"I find it a pointless endeavor."

"And yet here we are, dancing."

His fingers flexed around her waist. "Husbands are obliged to dance with their wives, no?" he said, his eyes innocent. Too innocent, to Willow's mind. "And you are my wife, last I checked."

A flush stole over her cheeks when his gaze boldly roamed over her. "And here I thought it was not fashionable for husbands to dance with their wives."

"Then I am most unfashionable." His voice was low. Amused.

"You must be careful, Ambrose, or people might get it into their minds you are doting on your wife," Willow teased. "And we both know you don't want *that*."

"Perhaps," he said, a knowing smile on his lips. "Husbands who dote on their wives get to drag them off to secluded corners and kiss them senseless."

Willow felt suddenly hot. Very hot. "And we cannot have that," she said. Oh, but she wanted just that. "So I'm changing the topic."

He chuckled. "Change away."

She puckered her brow in thought, watching him from beneath her lashes. "Surely you must have enjoyed dancing at some point?"

He pulled her a breath closer than was proper. "As a child, I enjoyed the practice, especially when it got me out of chores."

"Somehow I can imagine that."

He smiled at the dry note in her tone. With teeth. A real, honest-to-God smile. It was so unexpected that Willow started in his arms.

"It was always a point of great vexation for Celia."

Willow's ears perked at the mention of his sister, but she was careful to show no reaction except mild curiosity. "She loved dancing?"

"I could never understand why," he murmured. An amused expression crossed his features and Willow felt a curious warmth unfurl in her chest.

"Is that why you enjoyed it, because she had?"

"I learned because it was expected of me, but I *tolerated* it because of her."

"You must have enjoyed her company a great deal."

His jaw clenched, and he glanced away. Willow almost regretted saying anything. Honestly, why couldn't she just have kept her mouth shut? It was a ridiculous thing to say. Of course, he had enjoyed his sister's company! It was easy to forget, given the time that had passed, that he may still mourn Celia's death. That he would always feel bereft.

Just like Willow would always feel the loss of her mother.

All the more, Willow began to suspect Celia's death was the reason for his profound need to control the lives of others. What had happened to her exactly? A heart ailment, Cook had said. But that could mean so many things.

And she could not bring herself to ask. Already he was back to his old somber self, and Willow wished she knew how to get the other Ambrose back, the one that had just flashed his teeth.

"I love to dance," she chimed up, firming her lips into a bright smile. "It feels as though life's possibilities are endless when you dance, like you can dance straight into another world."

"Dance into another world?" he said, amusement back in his voice.

"Or across the sky and into another universe altogether."

"Now you are just conjuring things up."

"I am a known conjurer."

"Ah yes, you thought my brother a monster." He leaned in closer. "What else are you known for?"

"Whimsical notions?"

"Now that I find hard to believe." His eyes gleamed.

"Because I haven't fallen at your feet?" Willow suggested.

"I'm somewhat a legend in that regard, so it is most exasperating."

"I'll just bet, it must frustrate you so that your wife is an unmanageable heathen."

He pulled her closer and immediately heat bloomed, beckoning, enticing. Then he whispered five little evocative words that wrapped around her like silk.

"Less and less each day."

Ambrose had lost his mind. There was no perhaps about it. He was dancing, bloody *dancing*—something he never did—with his wife. Never mind the madness that had besieged him last night. But he'd decided not to dwell on that—overmuch—but who was he fooling? He thought about her every second of his day. And that was nothing compared to his hot and steamy dreams.

Which brought him back to the present. Why was he dancing? Because the waltz had struck up and he had this absurd desire to see a flush of desire on her skin again.

He resisted the urge to snort at himself.

Ambrose ought to be more concerned about the sudden flush he was feeling.

And then he'd mentioned Celia, a topic he never talked about. Ever. This was all Benson's fault for planting ideas in his head. He should not have allowed the seeds of his valet's words, of all people, to grow in his mind. As always, he hadn't intended to dance and as always, he did the complete opposite. Now she was in his arms, smiling up at him. And the worst part—he didn't want to stop dancing.

She intrigued him.

She challenged him.

She made him question himself.

Had he known waltzing with her would cause such a reaction in him, he'd never have asked. He'd wanted to see *her* desire for him, not go mad with desire himself.

So far, she had been a model duchess, holding her head high in the wake of all the stares and whispered speculation. He knew—or at least, strongly suspected—she hadn't read his rules. The radiant light sparkling in her eyes burned too bright. And like a fool, he found himself not wanting to do anything to diminish it.

More absurd sentiments.

His rules were in place for a reason. They were *necessary*. So why then, did he appear to waver in his resolve?

She disorientated him, that's why.

"You must have been the most proper youth in the kingdom," she murmured, drawing him from his thoughts.

"I would not venture so far as to say that." He had been quite the rascal growing up. Carefree even. Before . . . He hardened his mask. He had to keep his mind focused. "That was a long time ago."

"I have always wanted a brother. We'd have had a smashing time."

Her features lit up for a moment. Indeed, he could very well imagine her getting into all sorts of trouble with a brother at her side: riding bareback on horses, chasing each other in the field, and lighting fires in the conservatory. Smashing, however, was not the word he would've used. Incorrigible, perhaps.

Ambrose was suddenly struck by how much his wife reminded him of Celia. She had been just as full of life as Willow.

A disconcerting thought.

Alarming, really.

His shoulders stiffened, and his back snapped straight. He did not want to see the goodness, the once vibrant light that had shown in his sister's eyes, in his wife. It disarmed him. And that was dangerous. It would lead to a lack of rules, a lack of control, and eventually a lack of light. Just like Celia.

Though Willow was not exactly like his sister. Celia had been regal, a true lady. She would never have been labeled a heathen. Oddly, that comforted him. But perhaps heathens fared better with sickness. Perhaps the rules were now more necessary than ever.

The doubt and uncertainty ate at him.

"Ambrose?"

His gaze lowered to her eyes, saw the question there.

"Are you alright?" she prompted.

"My apologies," he murmured. "I seem to be distracted."

"Well, there is nothing like an eclair to bring you back to the present. Their sweetness solves all problems, you know," she said as the dance ended. "Would you like to join me for one?"

Eclairs. Sweets. Unhealthy. But he did not point that out. Because at that moment, she smiled at him. And he was lost. He was such an idiot. A lost idiot. But in that moment, he didn't care.

"Lead the way."

Chapter 13

The following morning at The Royal Academy

There was something to be said about a dashing gentleman forever frozen in time and neatly captured in a canvas. Not only could the gentleman be ogled in blatant regard, but one could, at the same time, imagine the gentleman to be the most charming of characters.

Willow was by no means an expert in art. She could hardly explain what she found appealing in any given piece that caught her fancy. Neither was she a dilettante but she did find there was something peaceful about admiring good art. For the most part, she just liked to browse over portraits to marvel at how talented the artists that painted them were—she never tired of the amount of detail they managed to express in their work.

Today, howbeit, Willow just wanted to clear her mind, and nothing opens your mental faculties and carries you away like visiting an art gallery. Alas, that was proving impossible to do.

Because her husband had decided to accompany her.

Willow cast a sidelong glance at him.

Must the man look so dashing? Like the gentleman in the portrait she was inspecting, he bled confidence and male arrogance. Unlike that man, who was leaning against a giant pillar with a charming smile, the duke was as stiff as a tree trunk.

Willow's gaze traveled over his clenched jaw before dropping to his hands. They weren't clenched, but there was a twitch in his thumb that belied his restlessness. The picture of a grouchy male.

A sudden urge to wrap her arms around his neck and kiss him assailed her. These days she was confronted with many such urges, so she'd become quite the expert in brushing them aside.

Her head swiveled back to the painting, her breathing shallow. Brushing them aside did not mean she was free of their effects.

Willow knew better than to fantasize about her husband. Unfortunately, regardless of all his faults, the man was tempting as sin. It was hard not to daydream and give in to bouts of hot fantasies when around him.

She snuck another peek and found his cool black eyes staring back at her.

"Do you not enjoy art?" Willow asked. Because really, she couldn't just glance away now that he had caught her stealing lingering glances at him. And honestly, he ought to have remained home if he was only going to sulk about.

"It's crowded." His brooding eyes flicked beyond her to the painting she had been admiring. "And how long can one stare at Viscount Granville Leveson-Gower?"

Willow's gaze traveled back to the portrait. *That* was Viscount Granville? She regarded the man in a new light. She would never have guessed.

"The man's a stuffed-shirt."

Willow shot her husband a look that said *look who's talking*. "I believe this was painted while he served as an Ambassador in Russia."

"Remarkable."

"He worked himself up from a second son to a titled peer," she pointed out, bemused. "That is something."

"And here I thought the man could not become any staler."

Willow bit back a smile, and then felt him tense when a trio of giggling ladies passed them. She turned to him and asked, "Why did you accompany me if you knew you'd be miserable?"

"I'm not miserable. I just don't find pleasure in gawking at paintings of men."

"Your posture is stiff, you are clenching your jaw, and you have a twitch in your fingers—all signs of being utterly miserable."

"Perhaps I did not wish to deprive myself of the company of my bewitching wife?"

"But what you mean to say is that you did not wish to take the chance of me slipping away to meet my sister."

"Were you going to meet your sister?" Black eyes scrutinized hers.

"I came to enjoy the art, Ambrose." Willow paused. "Believe it or not, I do possess a refined appreciation for culture."

"Of course you do."

She huffed and moved on to the next portrait. "But the more pertinent question, I suppose, is why you are tolerating an outing you loathe when you could have sent one of your lackeys to follow me around?"

"I have those? I thought they all answered to you now?"

"If only I can bring my husband to heel, then my life would be complete." She gave him a teasing look.

"And if only my wife would fear me." He reached out to place his hand on the small of her back and dropped his voice. "She would read my rules and life would be so much simpler."

"And spoil the suspense of discovering your beloved commandments from the utter vexation on your face when I break them? Surely not."

He inhaled deeply and exhaled a rich, completely mesmerizing laugh. She stared at him, fascinated that such a melodious sound could come from him.

She moved on to the next portrait, deciding not to break the lighthearted mood that had settled over them. They gazed at the paintings in silence before Willow's eyes landed on a portrait of two men who resembled each other. Brothers, most like.

She cast the duke another sidelong glance.

Dare she?

She might as well. It was impossible to say when he'd be in such a semi-charitable mood again. Her gaze returned to the portrait.

"You will not reconsider forcing a match between Holly and Jonathan?" she asked.

"You are finally asking me about your sister?"

His voice was soft, a mere murmur, but Willow detected nothing but amusement there. "She is your sister now, too. Just as Jonathan is my brother."

"In-law," he corrected. "Nevertheless, the brother you always wanted but never had, I suppose. What mischief will you and Jonathan get into, I wonder?"

"If he is anything like you, not much, I imagine."

He raised a brow. "Will you not press me about your sister?"

Willow shrugged, her gaze locking with his. "I am easing into that conversation."

He chuckled at that.

"Extremely unlike me, I'm aware, but given that I am bound to you," she gave him a once over, "and your moods, till death do us part, prudence might be more fitting in this case."

"Prudence, there is that word again."

"I've grown quite fond of it since our nuptials."

"Is that so?" he murmured, but a smile tugged at his lips as his gaze returned to the painting. "So you are not horrified at the prospect of until death do us part?"

"Horrified, no." Oh, the look on his face. "After all, you did not respond with a pompous remark and that is what I call progress."

When he stiffened suddenly, Willow's senses went on high alert. She slanted him a glance. But he wasn't looking at her or even aware of her probing gaze. She followed his line of vision to a woman standing a few yards to their right, viewing—quite arguably—the smallest portrait in the gallery. Her face was the embodiment of classic beauty: high cheekbones, plump lips, and porcelain skin. She had a wealth of sandy curls neatly pinned on her head.

Ambrose stared at her, frozen still.

"Ambrose?" Willow murmured, her voice soft with concern. "Do you know that woman?"

"I—" Ambrose shook his head. "No, she just reminded me of someone I once knew."

Willow's gaze fell on the girl once more and understanding dawned. Did the woman look like Ambrose's sister, Celia? The sandy hair, her youth, and her delicate frame all matched the descriptions Willow had heard.

Willow was not sure what to do. She wanted to comfort him. Show him support. She recognized a man in pain, and despite their differences, she felt that ache right alongside him.

So she did the only thing she could think of to show him comfort: she entwined her fingers with his.

Ambrose swallowed, heart in his throat, and focussed on his wife, who was examining a painting of a woman in a pose of reversed adaption of the classical statue, the *Venus de' Medici*, her fingers weaved through his.

He felt unbalanced. Unsure of himself. In dire need of a diversion. Anything to take his mind off the woman standing just within reach with the uncanny resemblance to Celia. And conversation was the best diversion he could think of.

"As a boy," he admitted, studying the lady whose hand extended to a white lily, "I dreamed of becoming a painter."

His wife's head angled up to him, her blue eyes glowing with surprise.

Then she smiled.

And the world seemed to stop.

Just. Like. That.

It felt as though Ambrose was staring straight into the sun. Had a woman ever smiled at him like that?

Lacking any artifice? He couldn't recall. Certainly never with such open amazement. And certainly not over something as trifling as a young boy's dream.

"I once, briefly, wished to become a botanist."

"You wanted to study plants?"

"Don't sound so surprised," she murmured dryly. "Although it must seem rather dull in comparison."

"Not at all but I still do not see the appeal of examining shrubberies."

"It's hardly all shrubberies. But at the time, the appeal lay in the prospect of traveling to every continent in search of various seeds and different plant life. Unfortunately, I could never tell the difference between bindweed and knotweed."

"There is a difference?"

Her laughter reached straight into his bones. "Of course," she said. "Alas, Sir Joseph Banks, famed botanist, beat me to it."

Ambrose chuckled when his wife pouted, drawing the attention of the few onlookers. He told himself there was nothing wrong with enjoying his wife's humor. Even though it felt as if he was dropping a thousand feet from the sky.

He cleared his throat. "There are more reasons than searching for seeds to travel the globe."

"Agreed. But at the time I was obsessed with exotic plants. Did you ever paint?"

Ambrose turned back to study the artwork on the wall. After a moment, he said "Yes, but before you get enraptured, it turned out I do not possess the patience to sit hours on end with a paintbrush clutched between my fingers."

"No," she murmured, teasing him with an impish smile. "I don't suppose you do."

Ambrose trailed after her as she moved from one painting to the next, balling his hands into tight fists to avoid taking her into his arms, which he found he suddenly desperately wanted to do.

That would be a much better distraction.

Something much like alarm lit up in his chest. A revelation hovered there. Something that twisted his stomach into knots. He hadn't realized that, by revealing a part of himself, she may do the same, and that he might see her in a new light.

Benson's words came back to him in a flash.

Damn valet.

An image of his sister, so pale and weak, raided his mind. A reminder of why he hadn't opened his heart to love.

This time, it didn't stop him.

Ambrose grabbed Willow by the hand and pulled her behind a sculpture of a young faun wearing a pine wreath and a goatskin.

And kissed her.

Chapter 14

Ambrose was kissing her.

This kiss wasn't an enticement or whisper. It was a demand, a bellow. His mouth was hot and exploring, his tongue boldly dancing between her lips.

A blast of sensation swept through her blood, thrilling her to the bone, and she lifted her arms to circle around his waist in response. She was pressed up so tightly against him, Willow swore she could feel his pulse quicken against her breast when she returned his kiss with equal heat, greedily devouring all he offered.

If there was ever a time to wonder at her sanity, it would be at that very moment, as they consumed one another in the National Art Gallery.

It alarmed her. It thrilled her.

When had the grounds of war altered to include touching, seducing, and an abundance of kissing?

Not that it mattered at that moment. Nothing quite mattered then. Not when his hand was slipping down her arching back, drawing her nearer still.

She quivered at his touch, tendrils of warmth wrapping around her. She knotted her fingers in his hair, holding onto him for support when it felt like her knees would give out.

He backed her against the pillar then, tilting her head up to deepen the kiss.

Only the movement wasn't all that smooth. Her back hit the pillar with a rather startling thump. Shards of reality stabbed at her brain. Even before Willow felt the bust rocking back and forth, even before she heard the terrible sound of marble scraping against marble, she knew what was about to happen.

Ambrose must have felt something too, because his tongue stopped dancing, and his lips tore away from hers. Their eyes met for a heartbeat, then turned towards the catastrophe. Willow glanced over her shoulder in time—so regrettably in time—to see the bust of the faun that had been perched so peacefully upon the pillar, tilt, and tilt, and tilt, and then plummet to the ground.

Her heartbeat slowed.

Their gazes swung back to each other just as the grim sound of an ancient sculpture smashing into a thousand pieces, of marble exploding against marble, filled the gallery.

There was a moment, half of a second, where complicity passed between them, and then he breathed, "Run."

Willow did not look back once as they dashed off, hand in hand. She did not look back at the grim event or the horrified people in the gallery. No, she did something far worse. She laughed. She did not know why it happened—lord knows it was not a laughable event. Perhaps it was the look Ambrose shot her right before he said *run*. But whatever caused it, the fit appeared from nowhere and once she began, she could not stop.

They burst through the doors of the Gallery and onto the slippery path of the sidewalk with scarcely contained relief. Willow skidded to a stop at once, doubling over from laughter, prompting Ambrose to skid to a halt, as well.

Heavy rain bounced off the cobblestone, the drops beating against her skin while she gasped for breath.

Within seconds, they were soaked.

Ambrose hunched down before her. "Willow?"

The sky rumbled.

"Willow," he urged. "We must seek shelter from the rain before we freeze to death."

She held up her hand, gasping for breath. "I know," more giggles. "Just give—," some laughter. "Just give," a bit of gasping, "me a moment."

"Willow."

"Stop!" She attempted to draw breath through her convulsions. "Please do not sound indignant at a time like this. We just destroyed a hundred-year-old sculpture and you said *run*!"

She was answered by a foul curse before her laughter was captured by his lips, his mouth attempting the impossible feat of kissing away her fit of hilarity.

Oddly, it worked. Seconds later, lips glued to his, she was lifted up against his chest and carried to the shelter of their carriage. She did not protest.

Knight in moody armor, indeed.

"So," Jonathan said, dropping down in a chair opposite to where Ambrose nursed his brandy. "Have you come to your senses or am I still to be married off?"

"I am in possession of all my senses."

Jonathan signaled a waiter for a brandy, pulling a pack of cards from his pockets. "The entire town is gossiping about your wedding kiss. I didn't think such a lack of decorum was in you, brother. I still cannot believe I missed your wedding. Rumor has it that the priest had to clear his throat to get your tongue out of your bride's mouth."

"I was thrown off balance," Ambrose muttered into his glass. "I reacted strangely."

"You've been thrown off balance for ten years, old chap, and you never reacted like that."

"What the hell is that supposed to mean?"

"You know what it means," Jonathan said, shuffling the deck. "Celia died, Ambrose. Sometimes people just die, and you don't get to carry that on your shoulders for the rest of your life."

"I have made my peace with her death," Ambrose bit out.

"Have you? It seems to me you erected walls—thick ones—around you. And the weight of her death is burying you into the ground. How is that peace?"

"And what would you know about that?"

"Like you, I carried her death on my shoulders. I thought I could have done more to help her, to protect her. I thought I could've done *anything* other than to allow her to live her life as she wished. It took me two years to realize Celia wanted her life exactly as she had it and that she would not have wanted that guilt for us. She'd have wanted us to live our lives to the fullest, like she did."

"I sat beside her bed for hours, waiting, watching, as she passed on to the next life, Jonathan. It tore my heart to shreds. Don't talk to me about what you think she wanted. All that matters is that I could have saved her. That I should have saved her."

"No, you couldn't have saved her, Ambrose. At best, you might have prolonged her life but not saved it. Neither of us could have done that."

Ambrose said nothing.

"And as a result of that weight of guilt, you decided that caring for anyone beyond mere acquaintanceship was not a risk you were willing to take. You erected your walls and isolated yourself behind them."

Ambrose did not want his brother to be right. But it was hard to deny the truth of his words. For the past ten years, things that had once brought him pleasure slowly lost all flavor and taste. Each year, with the weight of her death on him, he engaged less and less with the world as it was and instead, worked hard to shape it into what it should be. Worked on it until he had become a cold, controlling bastard with little else but his sense of control.

At least, some might say that.

"So I'm still to be married off?" Jonathan asked offhandedly, shuffling the cards.

Ambrose threw back his brandy. "Holly Middleton betrayed me."

"Only because you made her believe you fancied her."

Ambrose lifted his eyes to glare at his brother. Jonathan knew him better than anyone. He had always possessed the uncanny ability to see straight through him. "She wanted that fairytale. I gave it to her. At least, I did until I needed to explain what her new life required. And look at where catering to her fantasy got me! She ran off. What an impractical creature."

Willow isn't so impractical.

But Ambrose didn't want to admit that there was no need to pretend to be infatuated with his wife when he was quickly becoming obsessed with kissing her.

Jonathan chuckled, dealing them a hand, and pulling Ambrose from his thoughts. "Holly Middleton ran off because she had thought the fantasy *was* the reality. Your rules overwhelmed her." Jonathan glanced up at him, a contemplative look entering his eyes. "It is a curious position you find yourself in. One that suits you, I think."

"How do you figure that?"

"You are too tightly contained, brother. You need to unwind."

"I'm contained just right," Ambrose snapped, signaling for a refill. "And besides, how exactly does unwinding suit me?"

Jonathan arched a brow in response. "Well, for one, I can only imagine your lovely wife does not follow all your little house rules. I imagine some unwinding would help ease what must be constant frustration for you otherwise."

Ambrose cut him a glance. "My wife will follow the rules. Eventually."

If she ever bloody reads them.

Unlikely, that.

Jonathan smiled at him. "Does she know she is the only one subjected to them, that not even mother follows your rules?"

Ambrose glared at him.

Jonathan's eyes widened. "Is that why you sent mother to Bath?" He laughed. "It is, isn't it?"

"Sod off."

"Must be an annoying thing, for your wife to flaunt your rules," Jonathan taunted with a grin.

Ambrose grimaced. What was worse was that he was letting her. Christ knew why. But it wasn't like he could force her to comply—she was too damn obstinate. A trait he was growing too damn fond of. But then, his wife was anything but subservient. And he was blinded by the urge to kiss her most of the time he was near her. The rules weren't much on his mind when he was staring at her lips.

"I'll just go ahead and say it," Jonathan leaned forward in his chair. "Just let go."

"Let go of what, exactly?"

"Everything."

"If you are going to spout nonsense, at least make bloody sense."

"Give me a minute, and I will," Jonathan said, eyeing him over the rim of his glass. "Or not. You are bone stubborn. Of course, your wife seems to be just as—"

"Don't say it," Ambrose warned.

"Stubborn."

"You're bloody annoying tonight, Jonathan."

"Just want you to be happy, old chap. And you've got to let go of your control if you want to be happy."

Happy.

Willow's face flashed through his mind for the hundredth time. Could it be that simple? Just let go and be happy. He wasn't *un*happy. At least, he didn't think he was. But he wasn't happy, either.

What did he want, really? Did he want to be happy?

Suddenly, he realized he did know one thing he wanted; he wanted more of his wife. More kisses. More touches. More laughter. More mischief. More of everything. He did not just lust after her body; he *wanted* her. All of her.

Would letting go give him Willow?

Forgiving her sister might. Is that what Jonathan's twisted logic was getting at?

"What, then, do you propose I do?" Ambrose asked his brother. "Let Holly Middleton get away with humiliating me? Let go of her broken promise?"

"Why not? You got what you wanted—a wife."

"But not the one I chose."

"No, but certainly one better suited for you."

Ambrose couldn't argue that point.

They sat in silence for a few moments, sipping their drinks.

Then, unfortunately, Jonathan spoke again. "I wonder . . . have you ever stopped to ask *why* your wife married you?"

"To protect her family."

Jonathan clucked his tongue. "Do you truly believe one sister would run away without a qualm, but the other would marry you for duty alone? How unenlightened of you."

"My wife is more practical than her sister."

"Women are rarely practical when it comes to men and marriage."

"My wife is an exception. She. . ." His eyes jumped to his brother.

Absolutely had another motive.

Willow might not be as impractical as Holly but she was a Middleton. Their actions were never simply straightforward in his experience.

"Bloody hell."

Jonathan's teeth flashed. "Putting it together, are you?"

Ambrose muttered a curse. He'd not give him the satisfaction of his panic. He wanted his wife more than he wanted to breathe in some moments, and he didn't even know her driving motivation for marrying him. He, who prided control, was playing with unpredictable fire. More worryingly, he wasn't sure that learning her true motive for marrying him—no matter what it may be—would even affect his desire for her at all.

That should terrify him.

It did terrify him.

But he had a feeling it wasn't going to stop his pursuit in the least, regardless of the danger. He wanted more of her, full stop.

Ambrose glanced at his younger brother, considering him. "Why haven't you declared your refusal to wed Miss Middleton, eh? Are you not supposed to be up in arms, refusing to wed the woman who deserted me?"

"I wager half my savings that Miss Middleton will continue to evade your clutches," Jonathan's eyes crinkled, and his lips pulled into a smile, "allowing me to be merely entertained by it all."

"And if she doesn't evade my proverbial clutches?"

"I'd wager the other half on your wife."

"My wife?"

Jonathan gave an imperceptible nod. "To convince you otherwise."

"And if I don't give in?"

"Then I suppose I shall run away and live the rest of my days in destitution."

"Whose side are you on?" Ambrose demanded, setting his cards aside.

"You are trying to marry me off like a mother hen, Ambrose, and for no good reason, so I'm not on yours." Jonathan leaned back in his chair. "Perhaps it is time for you to decide, dear brother, what is more important to you: satisfaction for the slight against you—and let me remind you, I'm a key part of that devilish plot—or your wife, who will most certainly square the accounts should you succeed."

Ambrose met his brother's gaze.

"Do you want your wife raining hell on you for the next fifty years or do you want to finally let go of ten years' worth of guilt and fear?"

Well, when his brother put it like that . . . it was most irritating.

Ambrose rubbed the bridge of his nose.

He hadn't given thought to what his wife might do, hadn't considered she'd exact her own brand of justice on him. But now that he thought about it, there was never any question—she'd call for his head.

That didn't align with his single most desire at all.

Damnation.

Holly Middleton had thrown his world on its axis. She'd slipped from his fingers and Willow, who didn't tolerate his demands, had walked into it. He was losing control by the hour. Did he simply want Holly Middleton forced to his bidding to regain a modicum of control? Or just pride.

He didn't know.

And he didn't know if he could let it go.

But he did know one additional fact at the end of this conversation. A truth that had the added advantage of delaying this particular debate a little longer.

He knew why he married his wife.

Now he wanted to know why the hell she had married him.

Chapter 15

Anger pulsed through Willow's veins as she prowled the halls of her home in search of her husband.

Scurrilous beast! Rotten cad! Horrid ogre!

How dare he!

One hour after informing her maid she'd be joining her sister for ices at Gunter's, a missive arrived from her husband—a missive forbidding her the outing. The utter gall of the man.

It was beyond the pale. Worse still, he had sent a note, *a note*, to convey the order and, conveniently, he was nowhere to be found on the property—a property she was not allowed to leave.

Well, she'd see about that.

More than anything, Willow was at a loss. Today had been one of those days where, had she possessed a diary, there'd be hearts and kisses scribbled all over her husband's name. Revealing childhood dreams, kissing each other senseless and making off in a mad dash after knocking over a seventeenth century sculpture was the stuff of diaries.

It was almost impossible to reconcile this cold, infuriating note with *that* man. Four steps forward and eleven steps back. It was as though Ambrose was purposefully backsliding to a more sheltered remoteness—one where his heart was not exposed.

And to some degree, Willow understood why. He loathed laying bare any vulnerability. On the other hand, he made her furious. Was it so hard to include a reason? Adopt a kinder tone?

The answer to that was a resound *no*.

"Where is my husband?" Willow demanded as she entered her husband's bedchamber, startling Benson, Ambrose's valet. Her gaze swept the room, taking note of the dark furnishings and the large, quite enormous, bed in the center. Her eyes darted back to the valet, who stood ramrod stiff, a look of disapproval on his face.

Well bully for him. Willow did not rightly care what he thought.

"Your Grace, I believe his lordship is to be found in his study."

"I just came from his study and have searched every other room in this house. The duke is nowhere to be found."

"Perhaps he returned there during your search of him."

"Do not be impertinent, Benson. You dress the duke. You know his plans long before anyone else in this house. Where is he?"

The servant's lips pinched together. "I cannot say, Your Grace."

Clearly, he had no intention of telling her. Well, Willow refused to be a puppet that danced according to her husband's will. As things stood at that very moment, Benson had more privilege than her. He was free from any strings. He was free to leave the house!

"I must admit, I am astounded by the ease of which you lie."

Benson's face went slack. Hah! The man was not made of marble after all.

"Your Grace," he began.

Willow stopped him with the lift of her hand. "Are you telling me that the duke does not inform you of his schedule?"

"That is for his man of affairs, Your Grace."

"Yes, but don't you dress him according to that schedule?"

A light shade of red surfaced in the valet's jawline.

"Well, I shan't keep you from your duties, then. Do send word to my husband, wherever he is, if he does not present himself to me in one hour, I will leave, and I will not return."

She turned away. Let the valet stew on that! Of course, Willow could just disobey his missive and go for ices, but that would hardly send the message she wished to convey—he could not act the prince and then transform into a beast at a moment's notice. She would not be treated in such a fashion.

"Are you certain that is wise, Your Grace?"

Willow pinned the man with her most frosty look. "Do not forget your place, Benson. You may be loyal to my husband and believe yourself to be under his protection, but I am not an enemy you want to make."

"I only meant—"

"I am well aware of what you meant," she interrupted him. "I am leaving on the hour if my husband does not return. Who do you suppose will stop me? You, Benson? Will you tie me up and lock me in my room?"

"Of course not, Your Grace," Benson said, looking affronted.

"I am pleased to note you are more intelligent than that."

Turning on her heel, she stalked from the room, feeling somewhat like herself again.

She glanced down at the note clutched between her fingers, tangible proof of her husband's beastly side. She recalled the look on Ambrose's face when he'd revealed his childhood dream. How she wanted to kiss him right there in the gallery. And then, as if he knew her very soul, he had pulled her aside and kissed her. The world could have stopped at that moment and Willow would not have minded.

Willow balled her hands into small fists. Something had shifted. At least, something had for her. And sure, the primary reason she'd married the duke was to get with child, and that goal hadn't changed. But after glimpsing the carefree man her husband had once been, both while waltzing and in the Gallery, Willow wanted *that* Ambrose to be her husband in all ways, too.

She wanted the beast and she wanted the prince. She wanted all of him. And since that fantasy had taken hold, it was impossible to shake. She wanted love. She wanted a real marriage. She wanted a child.

She wanted everything.

Ambrose tugged at his cravat, staring at the shut door of his wife's chamber as though it was a hostile party. Benson had sent word that Willow had threatened to leave. He would never allow that. But it still set him on edge. She was his wife, and she was damn well staying with him.

He was only three minutes late. That did not keep his stomach from twisting into knots. Those minutes had, however, stalled him from entering her chamber. Willow did not make idle threats. And the only reason he hadn't lost his cool was that the servants would have informed him the moment she left the residence.

Inside himself, somewhere beneath the light buzz of brandy, Ambrose searched for the cold, controlling counterpart that had served him well these past ten years. The one that would serve him well now in dealing with his wife. How bloody inconvenient that part of him was intolerably silent, leaving him with a horrific case of nerves.

He gave the cravat one last tug and entered.

The first thing that struck him was her scent. Remarkably sweet, the aroma of flowers tempted him to toss down his boxing gloves then and there. Not that he planned to spar with her. He did not fight. He ordered.

That said, perhaps sending a note forbidding her to leave hadn't been wise. In fact, that had been Jonathan's exact words. But after being soaked to the bone just hours before, she wished to go for ices? It was deuced irresponsible. She could catch a cold. Which could lead to inflammatory infection. Which could lead to infection of the lungs.

Nevertheless, he ought to have chosen his words with more care, especially after the morning they had shared—a morning that left his head spinning in all directions.

Then his brain deserted him and he'd penned a careless note.

He was a marvelous idiot, yes.

But did she have to bloody threaten to leave him?

For a man who thrived on control, he had lost all of his. It had been years since he allowed his emotions to take command of his actions. Then there was the question: Why had his wife married him? What secrets did his little duchess hold?

She faced the armoire when he entered, hands on her hips, brows pulled together in thought. His eyes missed no detail, from the suitcase at her feet to the dresses scattered over the bed and the low fire burning in the hearth.

Bloody hell, she really *was* leaving.

"You do realize," he drawled, venturing further into the chamber, "there's no place you can go where I cannot find you."

She swung around to face him, anger flashing in the depth of those stormy blue eyes. Gone was the soft, powder blue he had come to expect from her—gone was the gentle pull of her mouth, replaced by a firm, unyielding line.

Her chin lifted a notch. "*That* remains to be seen."

"If you are referring to your sister—that is different."

"She still managed to slip through your fingers."

"Again, not the same. There is no leaving me, love. I will never let you go," Ambrose murmured, and when she slanted him a scathing look, he lifted his hands in surrender. "Not to mention I did not pin you as a woman who gave up so easily."

"Oh? And what sort of woman did you take me for?"

"The sort that slayed arrogant dukes," Ambrose said with the lift of his mouth.

She turned away and resumed her packing. "Is that an attempt at humor?"

Ambrose shrugged. "You'd have to remain in residence to find out."

A snort answered him. "If there is anything to slay, it's arrogance itself."

He clucked his tongue. "Fair point. However, running is not the answer."

"I beg to differ."

"Then run if you must. Attempt to make it past the front door."

"Oh, I will make it much farther than that," she said without sparing him the slightest glance.

"Not with me on your heels," he countered.

She shot him a glare over her shoulder before fully facing him.

Ah, now we come to the heart of it.

"How dare you forbid me to see my sister?"

"I did not forbid you to see your sister, I forbade you going for ices," he pointed out, his attention drawn to her lips and their soft, sensual arch.

"That," she spluttered, "might even be worse, I cannot rightly decide. But if you refuse me my family, I am leaving."

The words had an odd effect on Ambrose. Instead of being angry at her threat, he found himself softening. That alone caused his heart to slam against his chest with punishing thuds. He found himself drawn to her like nothing before.

"I will never refuse you your family, Willow. I, better than anyone, know how it feels to live without one of them." His gaze traveled over the scattered dresses before settling back on her. "Your home is here, with me."

She took a furious step toward him, high in indignation. Christ, she was beautiful—especially when she was spitting fire at him. She pointed to the crumbled piece of paper on the floor. He grimaced. Not his finest moment, penning that note.

"I get that your father forced marriage on you and I suppose I can even understand your controlling nature given some of your past. What I cannot accept is your note. If you forbid me the delights of ices, then you can at least forbid me in person. Which, by the by, is ridiculous."

"Not after you were drenched to the bone this morning. Not if you can catch a cold." His words were clipped.

"I'm much sturdier than that," she said, holding his dark gaze. "And if that was your concern, why not tell me in your note?"

Ambrose dragged an exaggerated hand through his hair. "My first reaction is to order. Demand. Command. Relinquishing control does not come easy to me."

"I'm astonished you can admit that."

So was he. *Speaking of admissions.* "Answer me this: why did you marry me?"

She blinked, her mouth parting and closing again. "You know why."

"Refresh my memory," Ambrose drawled.

Her brows puckered. "To save my family's reputation."

"And yet your sister showed no interest in saving your family's name from scandal."

"As you can imagine, we are quite different," she pointed out.

Ambrose took a moment to absorb his wife's response. Anger colored her features, but not enough to rile a real answer from her. He ought to just kiss her and pry the answers from her with his tongue. But she would probably not appreciate the effort at the moment, so he resisted.

"You are different," Ambrose agreed. "There is no disputing that—but you married me aware of the reasons your sister ran off. What did you hope to gain, other than saving your family? Am I to believe you are a martyr?"

"I became a duchess. The perks of my title are enough."

Ambrose gave a disbelieving snort. "You do not possess a social climbing bone in your body, so forgive me, Willow, if I remain unconvinced."

"That's not entirely true," she denied. "Every woman possesses at least one such bone."

"Mm, then why, since gaining the coveted title, have you shown little care or interest in the responsibilities that come with it?

"I have not!"

"Sneaking out in the dead of night?"

She scoffed. "That doesn't precisely unmake me a duchess. And what of your misbehavior?"

"*Mine*?" The thought was laughable.

"Your desire to control everyone *including* your servants."

"Hardly misbehavior."

"You find pleasure in punishing others."

"I assure you, I find no pleasure in punishing anyone."

"You threatened to deny my desires if I broke your rules," she accused.

"You desire me?" His lips cracked in a wolfish grin.

"I do not," she scoffed.

"Interesting to bring up that particular moment. No mention of toast this time?" Ambrose murmured. "Ah. Is that it then? You married me because you hold a torch for me?"

"Of course not!"

"Me thinks my duchess doth protest too much."

"I married you to save my family from scandal, that's that," she replied hotly.

His gaze flicked to the sheet of papers lying untouched on her desk. "Still haven't been tempted to read them?"

She cast him an unimpressed glower. "I'm quite happy ignoring them, I assure you. In fact, I should just rip them up."

"Destroying a piece of paper does not destroy the weight of its content. Or change the man who wrote it."

She ignored him and sauntered over to the rules, snatching them up. With a defiant glare, she crossed over to the fire.

Ambrose arched a single brow.

"I do not wish to change you, but neither do I want to live by a set of rules copied down on paper."

"You aren't living by them," Ambrose pointed out.

"They exist."

"That they do."

"And as such, burning them will make me feel infinitely better," she said and tossed the papers into the fire.

Ambrose folded his arms over his chest.

The sheets curled and burst into flames, the charred paper crumpling in ashes. She turned to him, her chin lifted high, eyes flashing with challenge. Christ, he wanted to kiss her.

"Why did you marry me?" he pressed, delving deep into her bewitching eyes in search of the answer.

"I told you why."

"And I remain unconvinced."

"I'm baffled, I assure you."

His gaze flicked to the flames. "I can draw up another set."

"And I shall burn that set as well." Her lashes drifted shut, inhaling a deep breath before they lifted to him. "I do not wish to change you, never that. I want to understand you; I want you to understand me. And your rules make me feel less than a person and more like a . . . jailbird."

"Jailbird?" He almost laughed.

"Yes, a person who has been imprisoned."

"I know what a jailbird is," he muttered with a roll of his eyes. "It's the vision of you, with a beak and wings, behind bars, I find intriguing."

She blinked at him in surprise. "Was that another attempt at humor?"

He shrugged. "If you wish for me to understand you, perhaps you can start by telling me the reason you married me."

Her hands settled on her hips. "Why do you insist on believing there is more to me wedding you than saving my family?"

"Your sister was brave enough to jilt me, uncaring of the consequence. You are no different. You married me because you wanted something in return."

"You make me sound conniving, selfish."

"I prefer the term artful."

"I'm sure you do, but that does not mean I had an ulterior motive." She turned away from him and tossed two dresses in her suitcase.

Cursing, Ambrose snatched up the dresses and tossed them to the floor. "You are not leaving."

She bent to pick up the dresses. "Why not be a touch more charming and permit me to go for ices and I won't."

Ambrose choked back a curse. He wanted to pull her into his arms. He wanted to hurl the suitcase across the room. He wanted to kiss her senseless. What the hell was she doing to him?

He just wanted to protect her. Rules meant protection—for them both. Why couldn't she understand that?

"Stay," he murmured. When she shot him a glare he lowered his voice another octave. "Please."

A faint crease appeared upon her brow. "Only if we can come to some sort of an arrangement."

"Fine," he bit off, as exasperation threatened to take hold of his windpipe. He shouldn't care so much about her letting him go. That would be the detachment he'd been hoping for, wouldn't it? Why then did the idea bother him? "Go have ices with your sister. But a footman shall accompany you."

"A spy, you mean."

"An escort," he snapped.

"Gunter's is hardly the stuff of horrors."

"It will be when you catch a cold," he muttered, his tone gruff. "Why can your sister not join you for tea, here?"

"I wish to go for ices."

"What nutritional value do they have in any case?"

"They are *enjoyable*, and there is value in that."

He shot her a hard look, sensing this was not a battle he could win. Not if he wished his wife to stop loading her suitcase. "Wear a cloak."

"Honestly, that is—"

"My final condition."

"Very well," she agreed, eyeing him with wariness and something else . . . Something that set his heart racing. "But I have a condition of my own."

"And that is?" Ambrose prompted.

"We seal our understanding with a kiss."

Bloody hell. Yes.

Heat rushed right down to his cock.

She stepped up to him. "It will feel less like a condition if we do."

His mind, his eyes, his entire focus was on her mouth. His hands reached out to cup each the side of her face, this thumb sliding along her jaw.

"As you wish," he murmured before he dipped his lips to hers.

Her mouth tasted of candied berries, ripe and sweet. She was leaning into him, digging her fingers into his coat, kissing him back.

It was almost too much to bear.

A sizzling current made its way along his spine when she wrapped her arms around his neck and pulled him closer.

Ambrose shuddered. The kiss was almost punishing in its sensuality. Somehow, by some miracle, he pulled himself away. It was one of the hardest things he'd done in his life. He wanted to kiss her again. And again. And again. And never stop.

"Go," he barked, clenching his hand at his side. "Before I change my mind."

Chapter 16

Willow paused beneath the branches of a maple tree, glancing up at the light piercing through the canopy of leaves. It was the perfect spot to meet with Poppy, and the fresh air was marvelous. She missed this, missed spending time with her sisters. And it didn't hurt that Gunter's was one of the most fashionable haunts in London. It would go a long way for society to see her happy, out and about.

"I will never understand why they'd mold something as delicious as this ice into a lamb chop," Poppy groused, stepping over a large root. "I prefer my ices in a simpler style."

Willow glanced down at her lavender-flavored ice cream, mounded up in a cone-shaped glass.

"I agree," Willow murmured, studying her purple creation.

"I still cannot believe your husband agreed to let you come for ices," her sister said. "I had begun to believe he had you locked away in a tower somewhere."

Willow shrugged, her gaze lazily following one of the waiters dashing from a carriage back into Gunter's. "I'm not a prisoner, Poppy; you really ought to come for tea."

"Is he still set on his diabolical plan to wed our sister off?"

"Probably, but have you heard? Lord Jonathan has always been in town. And I saw him yesterday and he is nothing as I imagined. The complete opposite from his brother."

"So he will not follow through with his brother's wishes? Or have you threatened the young buck with his life?"

Willow laughed. "No, I haven't gotten to that part yet."

"Just as well, threatening Lord Jonathan was Belle's idea. I vote for locking him away until the duke comes to his senses."

"Which might never happen," Willow muttered, thinking about her husband's stubborn nature, and then decided not to think further on it. "What do the gossips say?"

"Oh, the gossips have quite turned the tide." Poppy's eyes sparkled. "Apparently anyone who is anyone is gushing about a certain duke and duchess kissing at the Gallery and then fleeing the scene of vandalism."

"Vandalism!"

"Apparently."

Dear Lord.

"How is father faring with Holly's absence?" Willow cleared her throat. "He must be beside himself with worry."

Poppy's tongue darted out to lick her ice. "Oh, I told him she is well taken care of and waiting for the dust to settle."

"And he did not demand her whereabouts?" Willow asked, shocked.

"He did." Poppy winked. "I haven't cracked."

"And he said nothing else?"

Poppy shook her head, enjoying another lick of ice cream.

Willow sighed.

The fact was Willow felt a pinch of guilt at coming for ices since it was so clear Ambrose was worried she'd become ill from the cold. She could have spared him that worry, had she not been so furious at being told she could not meet up with her sister at Gunter's.

In truth, she didn't think Ambrose a tyrant—she thought him a man left too long alone with his pain. A man who had lost his sister, terrified of losing anyone again.

Moment by moment, Willow began to understand what drove Ambrose's need to live by such strict rules. The question was how to coax him back to the boy who dreamed of being an artist. It seemed to Willow she just needed to convince her husband that he could trust her, beyond any fear, beyond any doubt, to take care of herself.

"Father has always been surprisingly supportive. As for Ambrose, he is . . ." *An obsession.*

"Misunderstood?" Poppy offered, a hint of sarcasm coloring her tone.

Willow shot her sister a glare.

"What? It seems rather perilous to me to give your husband such benefit of faith. His actions have argued otherwise." She licked her lamb chop ice. "Then again, rumor has it the Duke of St. Ives is doting on his wife."

"You shouldn't be listening to rumors, Poppy. And Ambrose is not a beast. Not much of one, certainly." Willow paused, feeling a small smile spreading across her face involuntarily. "Except if you count kissing, we have been doing that a lot."

"You *are* doting on your husband."

"Am not! But I shall admit I enjoy kissing. It's all about exploring limits."

"There are limits to kissing?" Poppy gave her an arched look. "Well, you know what they say about men and limits."

"I assure you," Willow answered bemused. "I do not."

"Insanity lay at the end of a man's limits."

"That's absurd."

"What do you imagine lay at the end then?"

"Progress?"

Although, in Ambrose's tightly wound world, just perhaps, his barking at her to wear a coat *did* count as progress. He'd yielded, hadn't he?

Poppy made a snorting sound. "And here I planned on persuading you to return home if you weren't happy, but alas, we'd then be harboring a criminal, wouldn't we?"

"It was accidental," Willow said with a roll of the eye. "And I am not leaving my husband."

"For what it's worth, I wouldn't leave my husband if he looked like that."

"Honestly, Poppy!"

Poppy smirked. "Come now, the duke is astoundingly handsome. What woman wouldn't want to stare at his face all day long?"

"You are impossible."

"I'm envious."

"You've never clamored for a husband before," Willow said, tilting her head curiously. That had always been Holly's dream.

"True, but I do fantasize about muscled men with impossibly arrogant swaggers."

"Then go find yourself a muscled husband with an impossibly arrogant swagger."

Poppy waived Willow's retort away. "I have other pursuits I first wish to see fulfilled before I marry."

"Such as?"

"For one, I wish to partake in a play," Poppy said thoughtfully. "Perhaps write or direct one, as well."

"Acting?" Willow suppressed a laugh. "I shall wish to see *that*."

"Wouldn't that be grand? Oh, and I plan to commission a portrait of myself. To capture me while I'm still young and spirited."

"You make it sound as if you are approaching death."

"We are all approaching our death."

"That sounds rather macabre."

"I was going for dramatic, but macabre will do." She dabbed her tongue over the tip of her ice. "Can you imagine the backstage of a theatre? Surrounded by actors and dancers, the loveliness of that?"

"I suppose," Willow murmured, feeling concern creep up on her. Was Poppy lonely? She studied her sister over her ice. "Are you certain you are alright?"

"Of course, why should I not be?" Poppy inquired.

Willow shook her head, and was about to question Poppy further when her sister said, "I say, is that not your husband over yonder?"

Willow whirled around so fast her ice slipped from her fingers. It took two seconds to scan the streets before her eyes landed on the tall figure crossing the square toward them. Their eyes locked. The impact was so powerful the air rushed from her lungs.

"What on earth is he doing here?" Poppy asked, perplexed. "I thought this was supposed to be a private sisterly outing."

"I have no idea," Willow murmured, appreciating the fine form of his gait as he marched over to them. "But we are about to find out."

Ambrose stood shadowed by his carriage, cloaked in a jacket and top hat, his brows drawn together in a fierce scowl as he stared at his wife. The scowl, it should be noted, was meant for him and not his wife.

He made no move to interfere with her rendezvous, but listened to her laughter, such a sparkling sound it made his chest ache. He didn't know why he had followed her. He surely hadn't intended to stalk her. But he had been restless after she'd gone, and before he knew what was happening, he found himself across the street from Gunter's.

She was safe and sound.

He had thought that. . . What had he thought? That she would not return home? That Holly would join them? Or that she'd be exhibiting signs of illness from being soaked earlier that day?

With a curse, Ambrose drew a hand through his hair.

What was he doing? Account ledgers, estate matters, and parliament, those were important things. Spying on his wife? What trouble could she get into going for ices?

Ambrose shook his head.

He told himself he had followed her because there were too many elements beyond his control for his liking.

Bollocks.

He had followed her because he was obsessed. Plain. Simple. Bloody annoying. How can a damn man of his station be so obsessed with his wife? Her presence. Her scent. Her lips. It was ludicrous.

Who chased after their wife? This was the most powerless he'd been in ten years. When had he last spun so far away from the center of his axis?

Ah yes, his wedding.

And the night he kissed his wife outside her chamber.

Let's not forget this morning.

Right now, this very moment.

But the indisputable fact remained—his world had been thrown into chaos by his ex-fiancé.

But Ambrose had made his demands to his father-in-law and soon Holly would resurface. It would all come together, and his honor would be restored. Why, then, did he feel like he was sinking into a bog?

It was deuced easy to forget his goal—and how he had been slighted—when confronted with Willow's wide innocent eyes, the sweet taste of her tongue on his. And last night, his wife had the audacity to invade the sanctity of his dreams. Even now, he could think of nothing else but how her gown perfectly accentuated the rise of her breasts. It was impossible to forget the slope of her sensual hips, the perfection of her legs.

Clearly, his control had gone up in flames the moment he'd married the wench.

It was time to take back that control.

He crossed the street. Her sister noticed him first, and moments later, Willow spun around, eyes widening, cheeks flushing a pretty pink. She was staring at him in a way that made him rock hard.

He flashed his teeth—a smile meant to disorientate. She looked startled for a moment and then she stepped forward—directly onto a root. A stifled scream tore from her throat as she lost her balance.

Without thinking, Ambrose leapt forward, his arms reaching out to circle her waist, catching her in a dip.

The heat from her body seeped into his skin, and he was aware of every rise and fall of her chest. Their gazes touched, held, and neither made a move to part.

"Careful," Ambrose drawled. "You can hurt yourself falling head over heels."

Color rushed up to her neck and cheeks, and he chuckled. Yes, he was totally losing all of his faculties.

"You truly ought to work on your humor," she breathed. A bare breath of a whisper, but he heard it.

His eyes dropped to her lips, full and luscious, begging to be kissed again. He was a man always in control. Always. Control was what had gotten him through the harsh months after his sister's death. Control was what he had structured his life upon after it had crumbled to the ground. Control kept him and the people around him safe.

But every time his body connected with hers, touched her in any way, everything in him responded. Hungered. Needed. *Burned*.

"What are you doing?" she murmured.

"Breaking my own rules it seems."

He heard her slight gasp before he swooped down and crushed his mouth to hers. He kissed her because his life depended on it. His sanity depended on it. He kissed her as though they weren't at war. Or perhaps he kissed her as though they were. He wasn't sure.

But the detail his mind focused on was the wintry sting on her lips, starting a raging fire in him. A slow burn starting at the pit of his stomach. Hungering, consuming, and threatening to explode. She kissed him back as though her life depended on it, too. At least that was how it felt. Her hands skimmed through his hair, mussing it up from its perfect style, and he groaned in response.

He heard his sister-in-law huff. "Not doting on each other, my eye."

Ah, yes, they were in public.

He didn't care.

There was a long list of reasons he ought to loathe the fact that his wife's soft flesh against his had him leaping into a world of chaos—a world of broken rules. But the reasons faded away as he kissed her, until the only thing left to feel was how desperately he wished to broach the distance currently separating their bodies.

"You are aware I am standing here, watching you, as is every other person in spying distance," Poppy's dry voice carried over to them again.

Reluctantly, Ambrose lifted his head.

"Why did you do that?" His wife breathed.

"Damned if I know," Ambrose whispered back, out of breath.

And damned if he did.

Straightening, he carefully set her back on her feet. "Ladies, I'll leave you to your ices," he murmured, offering a small bow before walking back to his carriage.

Willow stared dazedly after her husband. She wasn't at all certain she understood what had just happened. His presence had been unexpected and confusing. Then he'd swept her up in a soul-searching kiss. Which in itself was remarkable.

Not the act of kissing itself. No, they had done quite a bit of that lately. But the soul-searching aspect. They'd kissed tentatively, flirtatiously, seductively, and lustily before, but never like this. Never like their very lives depended on it.

But it had felt right.

Intrinsically right.

Day by day, moment by moment, Ambrose revealed greater and more intriguing depth to his character.

Facets she found deeply appealing. Almost as if he was stepping back into the light, and suddenly, there were more dimensions present, ones she hadn't imagined he possessed.

He was almost . . . delightful.

"Is he whistling a merry tune?" Poppy asked, the question jerking Willow back to reality.

"I believe he is," Willow confirmed, having half convinced herself she had to be imagining the sound as Ambrose walked away.

"Well, I for one cannot believe he just kissed you and then walked off as if nothing happened. Are you still going to deny the man is doting on you?"

"Of course I am, because that was . . ."

Lovely. Enthralling. Deeply moving.

Something she wanted to do again.

Something she was sure she'd dreamed up in her mind.

"It's worse than I first thought," Poppy stepped up to her side, examining her flushed cheeks closely. "You are doting on him, too."

Chapter 17

Willow was *not* doting on her husband.

Poppy was wrong. Dead wrong. Doting implied she adored and worshiped the ground her husband walked upon. And that was not the case. Completely and utterly not the case.

Now, if doting had meant something along the lines of obsessed with or absorbed by him, which it did not, that would have been another matter entirely.

She entered the drawing room where Ambrose awaited her arrival a touch out of breath. They were dining together tonight. Alone. And her heart was beating a hundred beats per second at the mere thought of sitting across a table from him for hours.

Hours.

Her body exploded with heat at the thought. Well, it was time to test whether or not she was as flammable as she seemed.

Flammable she might very well be.

Doting she was not.

Slowing at the entrance of the drawing room, she found Ambrose standing at the window, gazing out into the night. She took a moment to admire the broad expanse of his shoulders. He made an imposing figure, dressed in cream breeches that hugged his powerful legs in a fashion that ought to be outlawed.

The temperature in the room soared.

Willow smoothed her hands over her evening dress of emerald silk, dragging in a tight breath.

Ambrose turned then, his eyes burning as they fixed on her. Intense. They are always so intense. Her chest expanded, and butterflies fluttered in her belly.

"You look lovely."

"Thank you." Gooseflesh prickled over her scalp. "I must admit, I was surprised to receive your invitation. You usually dine at the club."

He inclined his head. "I thought to make up for missing the last one."

"That is thoughtful of you," she murmured, entering the room. "I hope I did not keep you waiting too long."

He smiled lightly, his gaze falling to her lips. "A man is accustomed from a young age to wait on a lady."

"I loathe waiting on anyone," Willow admitted. "And I must confess . . . I'm perplexed . . ."

"By?" Amusement colored his voice.

"The Gallery. Gunter's. Inviting me to dinner. *Smiling*. You do realize we fled the scene of vandalism?"

"I already reimbursed the Gallery with a generous amount and no charges will be pressed," he drawled, his steady composure in clear contrast with the turmoil erupting inside her.

"Oh," Willow said, mortified when her voice came out as a croak.

He chuckled, warm and rich, and the sound sent prickles along her spine. He held out his arm, his grin turning wolfish. "Are you ready?"

"I'm ready," she murmured, placing her fingers on his sleeve.

That smile.

She found herself grinning back at him.

Excitement stirred within her, a hint of victory in its wake. *This* was truly progress. And though she knew she should be focusing on convincing him to let her sister be, Willow found herself thrilled for reasons far beyond that. She wanted to get to know this man, understand him. She desired a more meaningful relationship. She didn't want him to just be a means to an end any longer—a method to get with child. She wanted him to be her husband, in every way, to become her true family.

That did not mean she was doting on him.

He escorted her into the dining room and seated her at the table. A few candles flickered, not as many as she had lit before, but much more intimate.

Wendell appeared to fill their glasses with wine and Willow wasted no time in draining hers, motioning for more.

"Why haven't you broached the subject of your sister?" He took a sip of wine, his gaze watchful. "Pleaded her case in her absence?"

The question was so blunt Willow almost rocked back in her chair. He wanted to talk about Holly *now*? She wasn't at all sure if she was ready for that battle yet. Holly was still in hiding. Willow had time.

"Why have you not pressed me to read your stuffy rules?" Willow countered.

"And deprive you of the utter vexation on my features when you inevitably break them?"

"I'm not sure I appreciate your newfound humor."

"Not at all my character, I agree."

Nervous laughter bubbled up through her throat. "Next, you will tell me that you are giving our marriage the benefit of the doubt."

"Perhaps I already am." Ambrose lifted his glass to salute her. "To prosperity."

She raised her own. "Prosperity."

He swirled his drink in hand, tilting his head to the side. "How do you propose we settle the matters between us?"

Keep on romancing me with swooping kisses, to start.

"I hadn't thought you'd compromise," Willow admitted. "With your rules and anger for my sister."

"I might. If I understood the reason you married me."

This again.

She sent him her most innocent look. "What happened for you to become such a bloodhound on the subject?"

"You happened."

"Me?"

"Do I have another wife?"

He sounded so put out Willow laughed.

Then she sobered. "Very well, I suppose there is no reason not to tell you." Except her fear that he'd judge her too harshly for it, that he wouldn't understand, that he didn't want children after all. "I wished to become with child."

His eyes widened, and a flash of shock crossed his features. "You married me . . . to become with child."

"Yes." She emphasized her answer with a nod.

He settled back into his chair and regarded her with an unfathomable expression. His eyes were dark pools, impossible to read.

What was he thinking?

Her nerves pushed the next words out of her mouth. "Shocking, I know, especially given how I then proceeded to bar you from my bedroom." She laughed nervously. His expression shifted then, but she still couldn't read it. "But in truth, I've always wanted children and there you were, standing at the altar, and I—"

"It's not shocking," he interrupted. "Just . . . unexpected."

"Why? Did you think I had some other devious motivation?"

"I do not believe you to be devious." The corners of his mouth lifted. "An opportunist, perhaps, but not devious."

She lifted a shoulder. It was a fair assessment. "I suppose I am that."

He gazed at her a moment longer and she realized she was holding her breath.

"I am not opposed to children, Willow."

Something in her chest loosened at his admission. The fear she'd been carrying melted away.

Oh, good.

"I may have been opposed to marriage, but now that I'm married, I'm happy to give you all the children you wish." His lips curled into a mischievous smirk. "Even happier when I think of the process that leads to them."

Heat flushed up her spine instantly as she recalled their . . . process. She needed to change the subject. Immediately. Before she made a fool of herself by rising from her chair and throwing herself at her husband to initiate that very process.

"So now that I've confessed my secret, tell me, why did you follow me to Gunter's?"

"Would you believe me if I told you I found myself bereft of your company?"

"*Please*, give me more credit than that." She took another sip from her glass. "Much more credit."

"It was worth a try," he drawled with a lazy smile. "The truth is I myself am not sure why I followed you. All I could think about was kissing you."

Gooseflesh broke out on her arms.

Lust. Not doting.

"I. . . You . . . That is . . ."

"Rather unsettling?" he suggested.

Her eyes met his. "Unexpectedly so."

"No more for you than it is for me, I assure you."

"Is that why you haven't drawn up another set of stuffy rules?"

His lips twitched. "As you have not read them, you can hardly call them stuffy, now can you?"

"If they weren't stuffy, you would not be married to *me*."

"Then I suppose fate has smiled down on me."

Willow's brows scrunched together. "Are you *flirting* with me?"

"If you are frowning, I reckon I'm not doing it right."

The man was impossible!

And yet, Willow's insides fluttered.

Lord save me, I am doting on my husband.

"Why *haven't* you drawn up another set?" she pressed, trying her best to stay on subject.

"I have. They are on your desk."

Her eyes narrowed on him. "You shamelessly flirt with me and then you tell me *that*?"

"Does that mean I am crusty?"

Willow swore his eyes sparkled. She shook her head in exasperation. "I'm only going to burn them again."

His lips curved.

"At least explain their purpose. You owe me that much."

His shoulders rose and fell. "They prevent lack of structure."

"There must be *more* to it than that, this need of yours to control."

He flashed her another disarming smile. "What gentleman would resist keeping such a beautiful wife under his thumb, where he knows she will be safe and protected?"

"When you say it like that, it almost sounds romantic."

Laughter glimmered in his eyes. And something else, something that robbed the air from her lungs. His gaze dropped to the exposed flesh of her low-cut gown, and Willow was sure he could see her pulse leaping just there, beating away at an alarming pace.

"What are you up to?" The question leaped from her tongue. But Willow was sure he was up to something. He was acting far too agreeable.

"I'm attempting to be charming."

"Why?"

"Such skepticism. Did you not wish for us to become more amicable toward one another?"

"You expect me to believe you are being charming because I suggested it?"

His careless smile widened. "So you *do* think me charming."

"Calculating, more like it—devious, even."

He laughed. "Well, they do say there is nothing more honest than a man and a woman in bed."

Heat pooled at her core at the sudden intensity of his eyes.

"But we are not in bed," Willow pointed out.

"But we could be."

Oh dear lord.

No matter how hard she tried to draw air into her lungs, to reply with a witticism, she only remained breathless in response.

"You cannot possibly be propositioning me?"

"I promise you, Willow: there is so much more *honesty* for you to discover in my bed." This time roguish mischief did sparkle in his gaze.

"What about my sister?" she said, at last finding her voice. "Will you agree to let this grievance of yours go?"

Since he brought it up, she might as well ask. Before she did something as wanton as jump into his bed. He had a way to slay her wits. And that was just with a kiss.

He stared at her for so long, Willow thought he wouldn't answer. The fire in his eyes cooled and a different kind of intensity filled them.

She hardly took note of the food the footman placed before them, her gaze held captive by his, attempting to decipher every subtle change in his face.

Finally, he answered with, "I am open to discussing my initial intentions on one condition."

"Which is?" She could hardly believe her ears.

"Any discussion on the matter will remain separate from our marriage."

Her heart skipped a beat before galloping forward. She gathered his meaning. He didn't want their marriage to depend solely on the situation with Holly—not its success or its failure—but he was willing to discuss the matter. He was willing to listen.

Ambrose had just bent his stance—given an inch—a large one.

Her lips parted to say something, anything, or to just breathe. She wanted to dance on the table from relief and could not help the wide smile that spread across her face. "I agree that any negotiation on my sister's part is separate from our marriage."

When he returned her smile, nearly bashful in its presentation, her joy was suddenly replaced by a burning need to kiss him, to roll around the sheets, tangled limbs and all—in his bed. His earlier words had put a question in her mind, one which now refused to leave: Was there really more to discover in his bed?

As if he read her mind, he said, "And that negotiation is separate from the bedroom, as well."

Willow couldn't speak, but she managed a single solitary nod. When she did, his eyes filled with heat. Immediately, a mirroring heat bloomed inside her, beckoning, enticing.

For a moment, they merely stared at one another as the temperature of the room increased.

"Honesty is always a good start, don't you think?" she finally managed in a shaky voice.

"I agree." His lips stretched and stretched. He held her gaze for a long moment, and then murmured, "Are you going to admit, then, that there is the mutual attraction between us?"

Drawing in a breath, she slowly exhaled. "Yes, I shall admit that there is."

It took every ounce of Willow's nerve not to expire into a puddle as she made that statement, but the ravenous hunger on Ambrose's face was worth the courage.

His voice dropped an octave. "I'm particularly fond of your lips."

Willow felt herself flush in response. "I . . . I enjoy kissing you, too."

The moment was unbearably intimate. There would be no hiding from him, no escaping his presence from this night forward.

"But what of your pledge to withhold pleasure from me?" Willow asked. It was the whole experience or none of it. She no longer wanted to enter his bed only for the sake of becoming with child. She wanted to enter his bed for the sheer pleasure she could find there.

"That? Already forgotten." His look turned sheepish. "Not one of my proudest moments."

You can say that again, husband.

"Then it's purged from my mind, as well."

He gave her an unrepentant grin. "Shall we move on to desert?"

Chapter 18

Outside, the sky lit up as lightning crackled. Rain beat against the window and the loud roar of thunder broke through the sky. The tremors that shook the night were inside Ambrose, too. He could feel their vibrations, warning him that the taut, tenuous grip on his control was about to shatter in so many pieces it would be impossible to assemble them again.

To hell with it.

Ambrose didn't know what had compelled him to the concession that allowed his wife to change his mind about the fate of her sister, but he bloody well did not regret it—it had brought a smile to her face that had reached all the way to her eyes. In fact, it was odd, but he no longer felt as if a bog was swallowing him up whole.

He watched as his wife's gaze drifted to his bed. It was large, designed for a large man. He smirked. He couldn't help himself. He wasn't about to let her out of that bed for a very long time.

"This is your chamber now, too."

"You think I should sleep here . . ." She circled back to him, her tongue darting out to moisten her lips, sending a wave of lust to his cock. "Every night?"

"Yes." He couldn't say more than that, not with her looking at him the way she was. Innocent. *Intrigued*.

She had married him because she wanted a child. He'd never thought of children—he never thought he'd marry. But the moment she had confessed her desire, something warm had spread through his chest. Something that had felt like joy.

"And if I wish to sleep in my chamber?"

He took the two steps that closed the distance between them and slid his hands into her hair, tangling the golden strands between his fingers and tilted her head back. "This *is* your chamber," he brushed his thumb over her lower lip.

Her face brightened with a smile.

"Really, Ambrose?" She moved even closer to him, her breasts pressing up against his body. "You know how I despise commands."

The teasing note in her voice drew his gaze to her lips, and his self-discipline dissolved. He bent his head and lowered his mouth to hers in a deep, hard kiss of total possession. It wasn't enough. Would it ever be enough? Would he ever get enough? He didn't think so.

He drew back to stare at her. "You drive me bloody crazy."

He heard his own desperation in the words but didn't care. Hell, he wasn't certain what he was desperate for, except that in that moment, it was unthinkable not to possess his wife in every way. His tongue danced with hers, seeking more. She didn't protest his lack of constraint, and instead, entwined her arms around his neck and returned his kiss with equal fervor.

Wild with want and consumed by desire, he began pushing her back, guiding them both to the bed. Control was no longer an option for him, he understood now, so he just let go. There was no point in holding onto something that was shot to hell anyway.

"Undress me," he said, his voice low and commanding against her lips.

"Must you always be so bossy?" she murmured, but there was no hesitation in her movements as her fingers instantly appeared to shove his jacket off his shoulders.

"Yes."

He thought he heard her laugh under her breath as the buttons of his shirt came undone, and Ambrose wasted no time in ridding her of all her clothing. He tugged at her gown, and then at her chemise, until all of her garments were scattered at her feet.

One day he would undress her slowly and with all the sensuality she deserved. Just not tonight. Not after he had longed for this moment ever since the morning after their wedding night.

And Willow didn't waste any time either. As soon as his shirt hit the floor, her fingers were on the waistband of his breeches.

Ambrose couldn't stop a groan from escaping when she leaned forward and kissed the ridges of his abdomen.

The moment his breeches were unfastened, he tugged off his boots and stepped out of the confining material, sweeping her up into his arms.

He laid her down on the bed, the mattress dipping with their weight. He took a breath, his eyes searching her face. She was beautiful, her face flushed and eyes glazed with burning hunger. The tightness in his chest deepened and spread. Christ, what this woman did to him.

"Ambrose."

He smiled at the pleading note in her voice. Even the simple act of her saying his name sent a tingle along his spine. Dropping his head, he trailed kisses along her neck, down to the curve of her breast. He took a nipple into his mouth, his teeth scraping against the tiny bud. Warm and delicious, that was how she tasted. His tongue licked and flicked, and then he sucked harder. She gasped and the sound was sweeter than honey.

He paused, breathing in the scent of her skin—always sweet, always flowery—and tasted some more. He loved her scent. He loved her taste.

"You intoxicate me."

"More," she whispered, even as her hand reached down to circle his erection. Ambrose almost went up in flames. His body shuddered, and fire raced up his cock.

"May I touch you there?"

"You ask me that now?" He groaned into her creamy skin. He thought he heard her chuckle. "Don't ever bloody stop."

"What happens if I kiss it?"

"You don't."

Or I will bloody die.

"I want to kiss you there."

"No." He barely managed that one word.

"Please."

He looked up from lavishing her breasts, planning on kissing her to distraction and away from her current train of thought, but he made the mistake of meeting her gaze.

Her eyes sparkled at him. With mischief. With humor. With bloody determination.

He never stood a chance. He rolled onto his back and took her with him. She giggled in response. Shutting his eyes, he knew he should have just shoved into her right at the start because this, this was pure torture. He could feel her breath on his cock, hovering, looking, *and not* kissing him.

When it came, the touch of soft lips delicately brushing against the tip of his erection, he swore. It was unlike anything he had ever felt before.

"Have you ever been kissed here before?"

A strangled "no" lodged in his throat.

She kissed him again, and this time her tongue left a trail of blazing heat. Blood surged through his body. The breath slammed out of him. He was dying.

"I've never kissed anyone before you," he admitted.

She stilled. The loss of her was almost too much to bear. Why had he opened his bloody mouth?

He was about to reach for her, eyes fixed on her mouth, when she lowered her lips again, this time more boldly. And she did not stop. She drove him wild, her tongue dragging up the length of him, and her soft lips covering him with kisses. He was wrong. He wasn't dying before. *This* is what dying felt like. He could take no more.

Lifting her beneath her arms, he rolled her over and nudged her legs apart with his knee.

She protested, laughing. "I wasn't done!"

"No more," he growled.

"Did you not like it?" she asked sweetly.

"I bloody loved it, but I want to be inside you, and if you hadn't stopped, I'd have shamed us both."

She wrapped her arms around him. He kissed her throat, her lips, her shoulder; his mouth was everywhere as he pushed inside of her. She pulled him closer still, running her hands up and down his back.

He began to thrust into her then, slowly at first, until his body was no longer his own and his hips rocked at an unrelenting pace. It wasn't long before she arched beneath him and cried out his name. His own release followed seconds after.

His breathing slowed long before the rapid pace of his heart. The knowledge that his wife would forever be his obsession beat hard against the wall of his chest.

Thump. Thump. Thump.

Willow leaned over her husband, drawing soft circles over the rope of muscle on his abdomen. His eyes were closed, and a hint of a smile tugged at the corner of his lips. From what she could see, a pink blush suffused her entire body, likely right up to her untidy mess of hair, which she was certain resembled a pigeon's nest.

He had never kissed another woman before her.

The admission had been softly spoken, but it had hit her straight in the heart. And she would keep it there, locked tightly within, forever.

"You're so bloody beautiful."

Her eyes lifted to his, finding him watching her. She had to swallow to find her voice. "That is only because I'm naked."

"You are always naked when I'm looking at you."

Oh.

The thought of him imagining her naked all the time stole the breath from her lungs.

"That sounds rather exhausting."

A devilish smile curved his lips. "I have quite an active mind." He traced a finger over her calf. "Your skin is so delicate. So soft."

Willow moaned, barely recognizing the soft purring sound that emerged from her throat. "You're so wicked."

This man, her husband, had in a mere week stirred her more than anyone she had ever known. God help her, her mind and body ached for him. It was impossible to shake away the images of all the wicked things she wanted him to do to her. Even knowing he was a controlling, rule-obsessed man. Even knowing he was stubborn to a fault and that it would take a small miracle to get him to change his mind about her sister, about the rules, about how she should live her life. Even knowing all that, she still craved him fiercely. And if that made her wicked, then so be it.

He was once again on top of her, one large hand cupping her breast, his hard sex nestled against her core. He teased her nipples to tight arousal.

"We cannot possibly do it again," she murmured as his tongue circled the sensitive bud, sucking gently.

The way his eyes darkened at her declaration caused awareness to sizzle along her every nerve ending. "I beg to disagree."

She squirmed beneath him, and he entered her in one smooth stroke. A soft gasp pushed through her lips at the pleasure that tightened low in her belly.

Willow sifted her fingers through the thick, silky strands of his hair. And she knew then, wrapped in his arms, that she could be content forever there. The challenges they faced, the disagreements they held, paled in comparison to the glory of this moment. She sketched the image of them, just like this, in her mind and tucked it away into her heart. Perhaps this could be a beginning.

Tension coiled deep as he rocked inside her, thrusting harder, and harder, until she soared over the edge.

Later, when the damp sweat on their bodies dried and the air had once again turned cool, a wandering hand traced her calf yet again. A slow smile curved her lips, mischief on its edges. "Again?"

"And again and again and again."

Chapter 19

Willow wanted to be elsewhere. Say, beneath the sheets of her husband's bed. Like she had been the entire night. And morning. And afternoon. At this particular moment, even the library seemed like a splendid idea for a change of location. The cloakroom would also do. Even the linen closet was not entirely off limits. In truth, anywhere in Ambrose's arms would do.

Instead, they were attending a masked ball. Whose she had failed to notice. Her mind was all misty and fuzzy, and Willow had breezed past their host and hostess almost as if in a dream. An airy nod had been her response when Ambrose had excused himself to converse with Lord Avanley, leaving her with Poppy, who moments after accepted a dance from a masked gentleman.

Willow snatched a glass of champagne from a passing footman, aware a silly grin featured on her face. The bubbly texture and sweetness of the drink was just the thing to accompany her delighted mood. In fact, she hardly glanced at the tall young man who approached her, a wolfish smile planted on his mostly obscured face.

When she continued to feel the weight of his gaze on her, Willow looked up from her champagne flute, her gaze flicking over his silver mask. It covered everything from his hairline to his upper lip. He wore a black top hat over his hair. Did she know him?

"Can I help you, sir?"

"That depends."

"On?"

"Are you the Duchess of St. Ives?"

The corners of her lips lifted. "That depends."

His smile spread. "On?"

"What precisely do you want with the duchess?"

"To better our acquaintance, of course."

His voice. It was familiar.

"You must not have met the duchess's husband then," Willow murmured. For then he would know Ambrose would not tolerate a gentleman bettering anything with his wife. Her eyes traveled back to where Poppy was dancing with a nameless lord.

"Oh, I've met the scurrilous beast."

"Oh?" Willow turned to him, suspicion blossoming. "Then surely you would not be so wicked as to approach his wife without a proper introduction?"

He held a hand over his heart. "Ah, but we have been introduced, my lady."

Recognition dawned.

"Lord Jonathan?"

He laughed. "Do you not just love masked balls? They are so fun." He offered his arm. "Would you care to take a turn about the room?"

"Happily," she replied, placing the tip of her fingers on his sleeve. Willow's mind worked furiously. Now was the perfect time to bridge the subject of Holly and Lord Jonathan's intentions towards Ambrose's decree. If she could dissuade him from the marriage, it would be much easier to convince Ambrose to let the matter go.

"I must admit," he began. "I am beyond pleased my brother married a woman equally as stubborn. I do believe you are good for him."

A shiver shot down Willow's spine.

"I'm thrilled you think so. I'm also quite amazed you're not more concerned with your brother's plans to auction you off. That does not bother you?"

"Ah, yes. Must say, never thought I'd be the victim of an arranged marriage."

Willow scowled. "I cannot believe how blasé you are on the matter."

Lord Jonathan cast a teasing grin her way. "Two women against my brother? If I am not concerned, my dear, it's because I am certain you will change my brother's cast-iron mind."

"And you imagine that is wise?"

He winked at her. "I have lofty expectations."

"Let us hope your expectations are not shot from the sky," Willow said, her gaze searching for her husband in the crowd. "You know, if I fail to change his mind, there are other things I will stoop to."

Lord Jonathan cast a curious look her way. "I'm almost afraid to ask."

She smiled up at him, her eyes meeting his with unflinching regard. "You should be. So consider this warning: do *not* marry my sister."

"Or?" His perfect smile never faltered.

She let her gaze travel down to his nether regions before returning to catch his eyes. "Or you will be limping for some time."

He shuddered. "Christ, woman."

She tilted her head to the side, and her lips curled sweetly. "Nevertheless, you ought to know that I will devote my life to torturing you, as will *both* of my sisters. As will others who care for Holly. Shall I list all the people you can expect to partake in adding to your misery?"

He shook his head with a grimace. "No need for all that."

"Then we understand each other?"

"As clear as day," he murmured down at her, a smile once again curving his mouth. "You have sass, my dear, but for the record, I never had any intention of wedding your sister, no matter how delightful she may be."

"You cannot know how relieved I am to hear that."

"I imagine you are."

Willow nodded, recognizing the sharp underlining tone of his voice. A charming devil he may be, but Lord Jonathan was not a man stuffed with straw. When pushed into a corner, Willow could quite easily imagine him to fight like a dog.

They stopped at the refreshments table. "I'm afraid the cantankerous one has spotted us," Lord Jonathan said.

Willow followed her brother-in-law's gaze, and sure enough, her gaze collided with her husband's dark eyes. The impact was so strong it punched the breath from her lips. They bore into hers, hot and knowing. A warm flush spread through her body. There was no preventing rosy color rising into her cheeks.

"Am I to surmise from your pretty blush that the two of you are getting along well?" Lord Jonathan's tone was dry with humor.

Willow forced air into her lungs and tore her gaze away from Ambrose. "As well as can be expected."

"I suspect better than both of you expected. Just look at him. He resembles a bull about to charge."

Willow felt a smile tug at her lips. "Tell me, have you also received a set of rules from your brother on how to behave?"

Something queer passed in his gaze before he chuckled.

"Is something funny?" Willow demanded.

"Tell me he did not draw up an *actual* set of rules?"

Willow rolled her eyes. "Ah, so it appears that honor is exclusive to me."

"Indeed. I am not much of a rule follower, in any case."

"It is more fun breaking them," Willow agreed.

"Unfortunately, the fun is almost over." His smile turned rueful.

She looked at him quizzically.

"The bull is almost upon us," he clarified. "And he has eyes only for you."

He has eyes only for you.

Willow tried not to react to those words, but inside her pulse was leaping against her throat. Because she could not help but react to those words. Because she could not help but feel the same way.

She had eyes only for her husband, too.

Ambrose waded through the crowd toward his wife and brother, his eyes never straying from Willow's face. Candlelight shimmered on her pale skin, her lips curled into a small smile. Jealousy curled inside him, like a wave of swirling knives jabbing in his gut. It was entirely irrational, but damn it all to hell, Jonathan was the *charming* brother, the *likable* Griffin. Not anything at all like Ambrose.

He cursed at the direction of his thoughts.

From the moment he left Willow's side—and he had barely managed that—he'd found his eyes returning to her, again and again, wanting nothing else but to toss her over his shoulder and return to his bed. *Their* bed.

Thoughts of her soft body pressed up against him, his lips against her bare skin, her wandering hands shooting every thread of his control to hell were never far from the surface. Bloody hell, he had almost lost all restraint and taken her home, expectations be damned.

But he'd managed to keep his head about him, even if the impulse had been hard to control. He'd been content to admire her beauty and bide his time until it was acceptable to leave.

He slowed as he reached them, capturing Willow's hand and setting it on his sleeve. Her eyes lifted to meet his.

"Ambrose," Jonathan said. "Good of you to join us. I almost did not recognize you without your mask."

"Masks are for pups," Ambrose drawled. "Though I am overjoyed to see you are trading your old haunts in for more respectable events, brother."

"Nothing as mundane as that, I assure you, but since you married, these events have begun to hold more appeal."

Ambrose scoffed.

Jonathan motioned to the crowd in way of explanation. "You have the entire *ton* convinced you are the besotted husband. Splendid work, old chap. You pulled the wool right over their eyes."

Ambrose tensed. The urge to punch his brother swamped him. He did not require a reminder they were putting on an act, when, in fact, he had never been more in earnest. A fragile bond had formed between him and his wife. The last thing he wanted was for his brother to ruin that.

Not after last night.

Not after Willow had admitted to their mutual attraction. And certainly not after Ambrose was the most at ease he had been in ten years. He was determined to discover where their attraction, their dawning bond might lead them.

"The ton has nothing better to do than create wild stories to gossip about," Ambrose said, clipped.

"What about me?" Willow queried to Jonathan, batting her lashes at Ambrose. "Do I resemble a smitten wife?"

His belly knotted. Suddenly there was no one else in the room—only her, only Willow. She smiled up at him, and his heart clenched. And for once, he didn't give a damn. He welcomed the sensation.

"Oh, you are the personification of a loving wife," Jonathan said merrily, snapping Ambrose out of his spell. "Such a charming creature you married, brother.

You must be delighted to have fallen into the parson's trap."

"I did not fall; I was pushed over the cliff by father's will."

Willow turned her eyes heavenward. "Honestly, let that go already, Ambrose. Your father meant well in his own way."

"Listen to your wife, brother; it was still the best thing that happened to you, in my opinion, and me, since I was pushed into a hefty purse."

"You were what?" Ambrose demanded.

Jonathan shrugged. "I might have wagered that it would be a woman, not ripe old age, that'd bring you to heel."

"You placed a wager on me?" Ambrose bristled.

"I didn't start it. The busybodies of White's did. You were an unattainable bachelor; it was the best sort of wager. And I won a hefty purse." Jonathan waggled his eyebrows. "And now if you will excuse me, I shall squander my winnings at the gambling tables." With a parting wink, he wandered off to the card rooms.

"Well, I daresay your brother is a cheerful fellow," Willow murmured, her lashes lifting to him.

Ambrose grunted. "At the moment, he is basking in my misery. It will pass soon enough."

"You are miserable?"

He dropped his voice an octave. "When I don't have my hands on you, yes."

Ambrose loved how her cheeks flushed. Dammit, he was finding it deuced difficult not to cause another outrageous scandal by hauling his wife over his shoulder and marching off like the barbarians of old.

"Perhaps we could . . ." she cleared her throat, "explore the library."

He cast a faintly scandalized look her way. "I was unaware wives dragged their husbands off to ravish them in dark, secluded corners."

"Smitten ones do," she teased back.

A low groan rumbled in his throat at her suggestive tone. The intent in her eyes left him breathless. He did not even pretend that his control wasn't long gone. It was. Along with his discipline. They all just scattered in the wake of Willow's presence.

"I am thoroughly scandalized."

"A novel experience, I'm sure," she purred.

And then she was dragging him in the direction of the library—and he was happy to follow. Because he was sure there would be lovemaking, lots and lots of lovemaking.

Chapter 20

Ambrose sat behind his desk in his study and stared unseeingly at account books. There were numbers in them, which was as much as he could discern. The rest was gibberish. His eyes caught on one word: tenants. Yes, he had those. Tenants. Responsibilities. Estates to manage.

His gaze flicked to his disregarded cravat, carelessly cast aside over a stack of books, evidence his wife had been present not so long ago.

And what impact her presence had on him.

If desks could talk . . .

He looked over the ledgers again and sighed.

He could not even spare a thought to the people that relied on his quick-witted brain for their livelihood at the moment.

It was as if he was back at Cambridge again, staring cross-eyed at papers after a night of heavy drinking. Only today, he suffered no such after-effects. But he was drunk. Heavily intoxicated, in fact, walking around the halls of his home and over-imbibing on the scent of his wife.

His mind was filled with Willow, with images of her naked body writhing beneath him. And his mind had plenty of images to call upon. After their exploration in the library three nights ago, they'd since taken advantage of cloakrooms, darkened conservatories, and once, a linen closet.

And now, desks.

He couldn't get enough of her. The way she returned every touch with the same enthusiasm overpowered him.

He wanted to marvel in those moments forever.

He never wanted them—or this—to end.

Which was why it came as a chilling blow that it would, indeed, end. Soon.

Twenty minutes ago, he had received word from his men that they'd found Holly Middleton and were returning her to London.

Bloody, bloody, bloody hell.

The timing could not have been worse.

He ought to be gloating. After all, he had been right—there was nowhere his wife, or anyone else, could go where he could not find them. He had won. This should have been a victory for him. And yet it did not feel like a victory.

What it felt like was a devastating loss.

Ambrose pushed the books away with disgust. The choice ought to have been easy. Demand justice for the slight against him. Regain control over the chaos Holly Middleton had caused. Show everyone that rules—that agreements—could not be broken without consequences. And there needed to be consequences or everyone did as they pleased. At which point, society crumbled.

His brother's words came to mind: *You got what you wanted—a wife.*

Yes, he had gotten a wife. And technically he hadn't been jilted or deserted. Some might argue no slight had been made. But it had. And his pride had sought justice for that slight, his honor had demanded it, and his need for control had pressed for it.

But now another word had wormed its way into his mind.

More.

He wanted more. More of Willow. More of her smiles. More of her touches. More of this life he'd glimpsed with her over the last week.

No more fear. No more rules. No more resentment.

A dangerous bloody word, that "more," but it was also a word filled with promise.

Ambrose scowled down at the ill-fated letter he had tossed aside. How to deal with his sister-in-law?

Low and behold, as if fate had spoken, his brother sauntered into the room, his usual sunny self.

"Don't you look all flustered and out of place," Jonathan said, dropping into a chair. He stretched out his long legs and crossed them at the ankles. "Tell me it's not your reluctant duchess that has darkened your mood so?"

"I would hardly call my bride reluctant. She practically sprinted down the aisle."

"A gross exaggeration, I'm sure," Jonathan said, his eyebrows lifting when he spotted Ambrose's cravat. "Though, I am not here to discuss your duchess, but rather an update on her sister."

"What about her?"

"Where to start?" Jonathan pondered aloud. "Oh, yes, are you still planning to marry me off?"

"What do you suppose?"

"You know, as the second son, I always thought myself above arranged marriages."

"Have you now? You can go into hiding as Miss Middleton has done. Perhaps don a wig for disguise?"

"Don a wig?" Jonathan lifted his hand to his hair. "On this hair? I'd rather pencil my eyebrows. And you really ought to work on your attempts at humor."

Ambrose snorted.

"I've received a letter from mother," Jonathan informed Ambrose. "She is still quite put out about the horror of your wedding."

"She'll get over it."

Just as he got over it. Which, he realized in a moment of divine clarity, he had. Fully. Explicitly. Unequivocally.

"Perhaps you ought to join her in Bath and try the healing waters for yourself?"

Ambrose did not dignify that with an answer.

He glanced over to the damned letter, which held the power to snuff out his peace, and realized he held no true ill will against Holly Middleton. The pride, the need, that had driven him to pursue justice against her affront had all but drawn its last breath.

Furthermore, if not for her abandonment, he wouldn't have married Willow. And he could not imagine being married to anyone else. A part of him, in fact, deep down, may have been rooting for Holly all along.

Not that he would *ever* admit that aloud. Wild horses could trample him before he uttered those words.

But he *could* do something else.

Like, say, let his pursuit go. That, he found, was no hardship at all. Not anymore. Because damaging the ground he had gained with his wife by administering a consequence to soothe his pride would bring him nothing but misery.

"Your wife seems truly taken with you."

Jonathan's comment drew Ambrose out of his thoughts. He looked up from his desk to see his brother eyeing him with interest.

Ambrose sat up straighter. "She told you that?"

"No, but I see how she looks at you." Jonathan leaned forward, resting his arms on the table. "I see how you look at her."

Ambrose narrowed his eyes. "Your point?"

"Just that I'd hate for you lose such a precious gift."

Ambrose smirked. "That will never happen."

He would make sure of that, looming catastrophe or not.

"So you have given up dwelling in the past?" Jonathan crossed his arms behind his head. "To dwell on the past is to dwell on destruction," he finished merrily.

"Thank you, Aristotle, but I do not dwell where I do not belong, and I do not see how that has anything to do with why you interrupted my work."

"Seems to me I'm not the first one to interrupt you." Jonathan cracked a grin, nodding to the neglected cravat. "Decided to have more fun, did you?"

"That is no business of yours."

"I'll take that as an affirmative."

"Please don't."

"Loosen up, brother. Let past grievances go and live your life free of strictures."

Fate, indeed.

"Strictures are there—"

"To prevent your wife from suffering the same fate as our beloved sister, yes, I gathered."

Ambrose sucked in a breath. The pain stabbed him, sharp and quick, at the mention of Celia.

"Your wife will not suffer the same fate," Jonathan murmured softly. "There was no way for you to save Celia any more than I could. She was ill."

"We have been over this," Ambrose said quietly, darkly. The guilt he carried over his sister's death was his burden. For years it had served as a reminder of what happened when there were no strictures in a person's life. But it had been wishful thinking that Ambrose could breathe the force of his will into his wife. He couldn't. And he didn't want to.

"I thought it deserved another mention. Like I said, I'd hate for you to lose your wife because of our loss."

"But if Celia had lived a healthier life—"

"She would have died anyway." Jonathan shook his head. "She had a bad heart, Ambrose, and your wife doesn't. That woman's heart is as strong as her backbone. But you already know that. That is why you haven't forced your little rules down her throat."

Aye, that was the same conclusion Ambrose had arrived at. Celia's death aside, Willow did not have a bad heart. She had a strong spirit, a good heart, in more ways than one.

Ambrose knew that the day Celia died he had shut himself off from emotion, seeking shelter in cold, hard control. He'd done so because he never wanted pain to darken his door again. And so he had compiled those rules the day he proposed to Holly. They had been drawn up to ensure his wife lived a healthy, non-tiring lifestyle.

Jonathan's gaze fell to the letter on his desk, his eyes widening as he snatched it up. "You found her. You found Holly Middleton."

Ambrose cursed. He should have tossed the damn letter in the fire as his wife had done with his rules. And, admittedly, he should have called his men off days ago—only he'd been preoccupied enjoying his wife's touches and hadn't thought enough about how his pursuit for justice would affect their truce.

To force this marriage was the quickest way to make his wife loathe him. And it suddenly became important that his wife not loathe him.

"The men I had searching for her found her."

"And now you don't know what to do?" Jonathan guessed.

Ambrose glanced to the ceiling. "I know exactly what to do."

"A role of an eye. Have the heavens fallen? Or has your wife already rubbed off on you?"

"She is my wife; there was bound to be some rubbing."

Jonathan's eyes flew wide. "More humor? It cannot be!"

"I'm not a complete bore."

"You were." Jonathan continued before Ambrose could object. "But that is not my point. My point is that you *do* care for your wife. Maybe even love her. I can see it, old chap. So consider adhering to my warning and abandon those rules of yours."

Love?

Ambrose cared for Willow a great deal. But love?

"I can see you are bowled over by the revelation."

"Sod off."

Jonathan held up hands in surrender. "Only if you promise not to do anything remarkably foolish to scare off your lovely wife," he cracked a grin, "at least not without me to bear witness."

Ambrose had always admired his brother's carefree, passionate nature, but at that moment, he wanted to bash his skull in. But he didn't have time for that just now.

His eyes dropped back to the letter on his desk. At the moment, he had to figure out how to convince his wife that, though he'd kidnapped her sister, he was letting go of his grievance in order to keep hold of something else altogether more important.

Namely, her.

"Your cheeks are bright."

"What?" Willow asked, her eyes flicking to Poppy. She'd been staring off into the distance, fingering the rim of her teacup in thought.

"Your cheeks are bright," Poppy repeated.

Willow lifted her hand to cup her cheeks. "They are not."

"How would you know? Can you feel how bright they are?" Poppy said dryly.

"Don't be ridiculous. But I'm sure they aren't bright."

"They are practically glowing," Poppy said, her blonde brow knitting in a frown. "Also, you look airy."

"Airy?" Willow laughed. "One does not look airy. What does that even mean?"

"It means," Poppy said in mild aggravation, "You have the appearance of someone walking on clouds."

"I do not!" Willow exclaimed, almost spilling tea all over her pink muslin dress. Or perhaps she did. It certainly felt as though she was walking on air. Her eyes skittered to the sofa on which her sister was seated. She and Ambrose had thoroughly enjoyed *that* sofa. More than once.

This time she felt her cheeks pinkening.

Poppy quirked a brow. "*And* I am sitting in your drawing room."

"I don't see how that's related. I invited you for tea."

"Well, it's just another interesting observation. Have you forgotten whom you married? I keep expecting St. Ives to barge into the room and drag me off. Though how it is that you look so," she waved her hand in the air, "*airy* when your husband is hunting our sister and plans to marry her off to his brother, I'll never know."

"That's not going to happen," Willow said with absolute confidence.

"How can you be so sure?"

"Because . . . things are different."

Steamy different. Doting different. Airy different.

"I'd certainly say so," Poppy's voice was laced with skepticism. "Starting with that swooping kiss at Gunter's."

Willow opened her mouth to reply, but Poppy waved a hand at her. "No, no, you cannot tell me that was nothing. I'm still astonished Scotland Yard did not haul you away for indecent behavior."

"It was just a kiss," Willow defended, her face flaming.

"It's never just a kiss, and that, dear sister, was no *mere* kiss, that was a burst of fireworks and stars all at once."

Willow's hand lifted to cover her heart, and she forced herself to say, "It was a spur of the moment kiss, between husband and wife. Nothing to be so concerned with."

Liar.

If only Poppy knew what that kiss had led to and what Ambrose and she had been doing at every opportunity since. And that sofa she was seated upon . . .

Poppy made a disbelieving sound. "I'd have found it romantic had it not nearly killed two ladies craning their necks so much they nearly got trampled by a vegetable cart."

"That was hardly the case, and back to the matter at hand. Lord Jonathan has also assured me he has no intention of wedding Holly. He is on our side. All will be well."

Poppy snorted, but her eyes took on a renewed interest. "I cannot believe I missed him at the ball. Is he handsome? Tall? Muscular? Does he have a wicked reputation?"

"Honestly."

"Give me *some* morsel, a tiny scrap even. I'm starving over here." Her lips pulled into a pout. "With you romping in public and Holly off on a scandalous adventure, I'm bored out of my mind!"

"Oh, very well," Willow said with a laugh. "He is handsome, but not as handsome as his brother. He's tall, and I cannot speak for his muscles, but he does seem to be a charming rogue."

"Not as handsome as his brother?" Poppy said with glowing eyes. "I knew it! You have fallen under the duke's spell!"

Willow rolled her eyes.

"Yes! Do not deny it! I knew there was something different about you and that's it. You're in *love*."

"First doting and now in love? Honestly, Poppy."

But Willow could not help but be jolted by the thought. Poppy had been right before. Was she right this time? Willow was certainly doting on her husband and may even be considered *in lust*, but love?

"You must be imagining things," Willow offered, not ready to confirm or deny the claim.

"Well, you haven't put on any weight, so your glow must be love," Poppy murmured with a ponderous expression.

"Goodness! Why would I put on weight?"

"Well, when a woman is with child, she gains weight. You haven't gained any, but you're glowing. Must be love," she paused, then asked, "You haven't missed your courses, have you?"

"Would you shush?" Willow hissed, glancing at the door. "One does not speak of *courses* at tea."

Poppy snorted. "I don't see why not. Where else would we speak of them? It's the natural course of a marriage."

"Well my courses are just fine."

Speaking of which, when had motherhood become the furthest thing from her mind? A doting mama was all she'd ever wanted to be. Instead she was doting on her husband.

A startling thought.

Children were the very reason she had married Ambrose. And yet, at the moment, the longing, the constant yearning had subsided. She still wanted to be a mother, but she was enjoying the intimacy she shared with her husband. Which might very likely lead to her being *enceinte*.

All was good with the world.

She sat stunned, teacup tightly clasped in her hand, marveling.

All *was* good with the world.

The only thing that remained was to ask her husband to let go of his disgruntlement, for her, for them, which she was certain he had already done, and the world would be perfect.

Something magical had exploded into her life.

Something much like love.

Maybe Poppy was right.

Maybe there was something different about her, after all.

Chapter 21

Ambrose stared down at Holly Middleton with hard eyes. He was sure his face was expressionless, and he kept his mask in place even though inside he was rock steady. His sister-in-law had caused him quite some trouble, not to mention had almost cost him his entire inheritance. She was also the woman whose actions had given him his wife.

Needless to say, his feelings on Holly Middleton were not as conflicted as before. They were quite simple. He would not lose his wife now that he'd found her. Anything else qualified as insignificance.

And Ambrose was painfully aware that, if he wasn't careful in the way he handled this devil of a situation with her sister, Willow might leave.

Just thinking about how his wife might react if he wasn't careful had him fighting the urge to tug at his cravat.

Miss Middleton's eyes fluttered open.

"Good, you are awake." He saw her wince. She looked so damn much like her sister, it almost hurt to look at her. He'd throttle an imbecile who dared kidnap Willow. It chafed knowing that at the moment, he was that imbecile.

"You found me; you must be in raptures," she said, her voice still thick from sleep.

Ambrose recalled that the men had said they'd given her a dose of laudanum after she had attempted to escape them. She had also been hurt in her attempt to escape. He had released his fury upon the men over that. He hadn't wanted Miss Middleton hurt. He'd merely wanted her present to account for her actions and now he didn't even want that. He just wanted this matter to be done with. He already felt too much like a bastard.

"Did you truly think I would not? Did you truly believe jilting me would not carry any consequence?" Ambrose could at least make a point about consequences and all that. Perhaps *some* of it would sink in before he released her in the morning.

She *had* betrayed him, after all. Though, not before he'd done the same, admittedly, given that he might have allowed her to believe he found her attractive and possessed affection for her—neither of which had been true.

But that was no longer important.

The scene had been set. He'd wake his wife with his lips and every other part of his body. They'd make love. After they'd worked up an appetite, they'd go down for breakfast. At the table, Willow would find a feast spread out. And her sister. At which point he declared all animosity in the past. And apologize for his part in her running off.

It seemed today was a day for all sorts of revelations and self-reflection, including that he'd been an ass *first*.

And he'd be remiss if he denied that, for a moment, he missed the cold control that had allowed him to feel nothing for the last decade.

"Yes, yes, you are a mighty duke and shall deliver my comeuppance. Spare me the woeful tale of how my betrayal forever broke your heart. You married my sister. That is a far cry from being jilted. In fact, if I am to believe the *London Times*, you always meant to marry Willow, not me."

Ambrose clenched his jaw. Christ Almighty, save him from women. Clearly, she did not regret her behavior. In fact, she'd already justified it.

He let out a deep breath. "A necessary tale to spare both our houses the humiliation of your actions."

"It seems like everything worked out for you, Your Grace, so why must you still do this?"

Ambrose paused. Should he tell her now?

No, he had a plan, one with a sequence of events. Well thought out events. And with some luck, after a night to ponder the consequences of what she'd done, Holly might pause and reflect before her next harebrained adventure.

God willing.

"You embarrassed my family," Ambrose pointed out. "You gave your word and then you broke it."

"And what of you?" she challenged. "You hid your true feelings, masked your true intentions. What is that if not breaking one's word? And now I must be the one punished? You have no right to me, Your Grace. I am not yours."

Thank God for that.

"You made sure of that, did you not, Miss Middleton? But there are other ways to mete out lessons."

Like stewing on the idea that she was being held prisoner, awaiting a doomed fate.

Twelve hours wouldn't make much of a difference in the grand scheme of things. It also gave him time to polish the finer details of his plan. And *that* was important. Because he needed Willow to understand he had harmonized his view of their marriage, his ways, and his past—that he wanted nothing but her happiness.

"A lesson is one thing, marriage to your brother is lifelong," she pointed out.

"So that is why you ran away instead of facing the aftermath of your actions, the threat of another looming marriage."

"I'm curious, what does Lord Jonathan have to say about this plan of yours? What has he done to warrant the same punishment as me?"

"It's past time he marries," Ambrose murmured. That wasn't untrue, he supposed.

"So you will happily doom us both to a life of unhappiness?"

He'd been willing to, hadn't he? And then his wife had changed everything with her smart mouth, lingering touches, and bright smile. She had cast her own light on him.

In that moment, staring down into his sister-in-law's face, Ambrose felt truly grateful for the upheaval of his life. He'd been such a bloody ass before.

"You betrayed me," he said simply.

"Your brother did not."

Ambrose stopped his lips from curving into a sly smile. For the first time since they met, he admired Holly Middleton's spunk. She didn't have as much as her sister, in his opinion, and she also didn't look as beautiful as his wife did in her ire, but he admired it nonetheless.

"How can you believe what you did was right?" Miss Middleton continued to demand. "That it was acceptable to deceive me and fool me into believing you were something you were clearly not?"

Because I was different then. And desperate.

"We all put our best self forward when making new acquaintances, Miss Middleton," Ambrose drawled instead.

"*That* was your best self?"

"I was being charming."

"Up till the moment you handed me a set of rules to live by. You really ought to have waited until after the wedding."

"Agreed."

Though he was glad he hadn't. He'd never thought he'd be glad that Holly Middleton had abandoned him at the altar, but he was in bloody raptures.

"I am a person, you know," she snapped. "Not a slave. I do not need my meals assigned to me. Your deception went too far. Your rules go too far."

Ambrose was tempted to throw his hands up in a rant. His rules were ridiculous, he got the bloody message. Exasperated at everyone's opinion, he ground out, "The rules are there for a reason."

"Reasons that apparently do not require any explanation. How is my dear sister faring with those rules?"

"Your sister is . . ." Wonderful. Beautiful. Infuriating. "A challenge," he muttered.

"Have you ever considered that your rules suppress the very essence of our nature?"

Of course he had. It was one of the reasons he had never pressed Willow to follow them—not truly.

"Because it is not in your nature to follow rules?" he asked.

"It's not our way to blindly follow," she corrected. "If I were you, Your Grace, I'd focus on what does lie in our nature rather than on what doesn't. Your life would be easier."

Now his sister-in-law was dispensing marital advice? They'd veered too far off topic. Refocus and wrap things up. He had things to plan. That and this berating was beginning to get deuced uncomfortable.

"Wise advice, but it changes nothing. You will marry Jonathan."

"Are you in possession of a heart? Do you feel anything resembling emotion, or is this all just a pretense?"

At the present, mostly pretense. Though not the sort she was talking about, he was sure.

"Oh, I feel," Ambrose declared. "I feel too damn much." More than she, his wife, or his brother could ever suspect. "And it changes nothing. You will marry my brother within the coming fortnight and become part of the family you so wished to escape from."

Inside, a smile spread. Outside he remained remarkably poised. Perhaps in his next life he could try his hand at acting.

"I am already part of your family! Is that not enough?"

"My decision has been made."

It took effort to keep his mask in place, as saying it out loud nearly made him smile. The shock on her face tomorrow morning would be priceless. He bit down on his jaw.

"You tricked me! You used my romantic ideals against me from the beginning! You sought to take advantage of my nature, which ought to be punishment enough."

It was on the tip of his tongue to tell her to go. To run home or to run to Willow. He nipped the urge in the bud. He had to speak to his wife first.

"It was imperative that I marry posthaste, and you were in desperate need of falling in love," he found himself admitting. Here and now, he could give Holly Middleton this one honesty.

"Not that desperate."

He almost chuckled at her waspish tone. "I miscalculated."

"You thought me too weak to oppose you."

"Not weak, Miss Middleton, only smart."

"Where is my sister?" she countered. "I wish to see her."

"All in good time."

"Too afraid we will outsmart you once again?"

They likely would if he had any intention of staying this course.

"Precautionary measures."

"But of course."

"As you said, Miss Middleton, I should focus on what lies in your nature. You can't help but stir trouble."

"Does Willow know you are keeping me against my will?"

"My wife knows what I see fit to tell her." Christ, he sounded like a jackass. He couldn't wait until the ruse was up.

He suddenly recalled his men saying that she had to have had help in running away.

"Have you been compromised?" he asked, his sudden concern startling him. It shouldn't have, however. She was Willow's family, which made her his family, too.

"You sent three monkeys after me."

"A simple yes or no would suffice." His men hadn't touched her, he knew that much, but he gave her credit for that strategy.

"Yes," she snapped.

Ambrose did allow his lips to curve into a smile then. "I see your spirit hasn't been broken by your little adventure. I am, however, disinclined to believe you."

"Then why did you ask?"

Best not answer that one.

"The men that brought you back told me of your little attempt to escape and that you were thrown from your horse in the effort."

"I've had rotten luck lately."

"They spoke the truth, then?"

"Yes, though you'll believe nothing I say in any case."

"They also told me you were aided by a gentleman."

"A tale I told in an attempt to foil them."

No, there had been someone. Her eyes told him so.

"You are a terrible liar, Miss Middleton," Ambrose drawled. "Your eyes are much too expressive. If there was indeed a man who aided you, I will discover his identity and bring him to task."

Or, more likely, drag him to the altar to marry her. They were now family, after all. God help him.

"You are under the mistaken impression that every man quakes in his boots at the prospect of defying you."

"Some men are brave," he agreed.

"Some men, Your Grace, are more formidable than you give them credit for. And some are far more dangerous than even yourself."

"A man is only as formidable as the friends that stand at his back, Miss Middleton."

"And how many people stand at yours, Your Grace?"

"Friends come in all forms, Miss Middleton." He stood. A menu for breakfast awaited his attention. "If you will excuse me, I have preparations to see to."

"What of my father? You cannot marry me against my will!"

"Your father has given his permission to the union." It was a blatant lie, but it served his purpose. Oil to the fire.

"That is a lie! He would never do that!"

Ambrose turned on his heel and stalked from the room. He had said all he had come to say. But mostly he had wanted to see for himself whether resentment coiled in his gut at the sight of her.

It hadn't.

In fact, he looked forward to dropping the ruse and seeing Willow's smile when he did.

A grin curved his lips.

Willow was daydreaming. Again. It had become quite the habit, one she enjoyed rather immensely. And, at the moment, she was daydreaming about how she was planning to seduce her husband, thoroughly, completely, and (this was the most important part) wicked, wicked, wickedly tonight.

There was only one problem.

She lifted her nightgown, holding it up before her for inspection.

It was, in a word, revolting. Utterly unbecoming. Downright repellant. Nothing one would wear to a seduction, especially when said seduction was the prelude to getting one's husband in a good mood to talk about all the reasons he ought to drop this score he wished to settle with her sister.

She stared at the nightgown. If she wore it, every inch of her flesh would be covered. *And* it was yellow. Ish. Her nose wrinkled. So, no, she hadn't planned her nightwear to include marriage or seduction, but this particular travesty was shameful. Shameful, albeit comfortable to sleep in.

Well, she couldn't wear it.

I could always wait for him naked.

The thought started up all sorts of wicked memories.

Willow shivered.

She flung the garment to the side. She would wait naked. Under the covers. In any case, shyness was no longer an option. Not after she had brazenly kissed him *there*.

Heavens! She couldn't think about that and not feel heated.

Perhaps she ought to open a window and allow for some crisp air to breathe into the room and soothe the warmth of her skin.

Ah yes, that did sound lovely.

With that marvelous idea in mind, she quickly did just that, delighted when the soft rays of the moonlight cast the walnut floor in a wildly romantic glow.

Shedding her clothes, Willow settled under the covers to wait.

Chapter 22

Ambrose stared down at his sleeping wife in wondering fascination, tracing the side of her face with a gentle finger. The room was dark with only a few embers still illuminating the bed in a soft glow. He drew in a deep breath, inhaling the scent of her sweetness into his lungs. Her hair fanned over his shoulder where her head rested, soft and silky. She looked so sweet and innocent in her sleep; her beauty tore at his heart.

Ambrose hadn't expected to find happiness or even a measure of joy in his marriage. And the truth was that he hadn't tried all that hard. He had been nothing but a beast ever since he set out to find a wife, had thought only of himself and his resentment towards his father.

His wife's words came to mind. *Let it go already . . . Your father meant well in his own way.*

His wife was right. Whatever Ambrose's thoughts might be over the clause, his father's intentions had come from a place in his heart. A strange place. But a place in that region, nonetheless.

In a way, Ambrose was much like the late duke, who had also valued structure and order. His heir was his heir. There was no spare for the spare. And yes, Ambrose had gone overboard with his sense of protection after Celia's death, but he was working on that.

And even after all that, a miracle had still landed on his lap. A miracle within a miracle. A miracle that drew him in and slayed the beast inside him with every look.

That he felt happiness now scared the hell out of him. He was in a constant flustered state.

And the fact that he held her sister prisoner at the moment was deuced foolish. Yes, in a few short hours she'd be free, but he still felt like a royal bastard.

Maybe he should wake his wife and simply tell her now. He stroked his fingers through her silky strands, studying her face. She was sleeping so soundly, he couldn't bear to wake her.

Only a few more hours.

He pressed a soft kiss to Willow's temple, his lips lingering against her skin.

She might still be furious with him for not informing her sooner, but Ambrose was confident he could cross that bridge unscathed. After all, in the end, he'd done the right thing. His heart was in the right place. His heart was with her.

Closing his eyes, he savored this moment with her in his arms, and felt himself drifting off to sleep.

The sudden shout of a muffled voice from somewhere in the house snapped him back to alertness. He slowly pulled away from his wife.

Warning flared in his gut—trouble.

He planted a soft kiss on the tip of her nose before leaving the bed.

He barely cleared the chamber before the unmistakable boom of his name vibrated through the halls.

"St. Ives!"

"Get your rotten ass down here or I'll tear this place apart," the voice blustered.

"St. Ives!"

Ambrose quickened his steps, mindful that the shouts could wake Willow at any moment. Displeasure, annoyance, and anger consumed him all at once. Who the hell dared to enter his home in such a shockingly improper manner?

He halted in the center of the stairwell and could not believe his bloody eyes. The Marquis of Warton stood in the front hall, his eyes colliding with his like a flash of thunder. Warton was all but frothing at the mouth.

Had the world gone to hell?

"What the devil is the meaning of this?" Ambrose demanded. His voice cold and laced with steel.

Behind him the air shifted, the sweet scent alerting him to the arrival of his wife. Tension curled in his chest. He dared not look back at her.

"Where the hell is she?" Warton growled.

Ambrose stiffened. His heart thudded so hard a light whir began to ring in his ears.

Behind him, his wife gasped.

And in that gasp, he heard it. Willow knew. She'd known the whereabouts of her sister all along. Had known Warton was involved, too.

Of course, he had suspected she'd met with her sister the night he discovered her sneaking out of their home, but he hadn't expected this brutal blow to his gut on learning she'd kept it from him. Then again, he had been on the path of justness at the time.

Warton, however, Ambrose hadn't seen that coming at all. And now the man was making a scene in front of his wife.

Fury gripped his gut.

How dare this man enter his home in such a fashion?

"So you are the one who aided my wayward sister-in-law with her escape," Ambrose drawled.

"And you are the controlling bastard who won't afford his wife the pleasure of an extra piece of toast."

Christ, the toast again.

Had anyone cared to ask him, he would have told them the content of Cook's bread was highly nutritional and no more than one slice was required for nourishment. In fact, more than one slice would swiftly plump you up.

"Not to mention an inglorious cur that sent three mercenary riders to snatch up a lady."

Willow's sharp intake of breath inflamed Ambrose's temper towards Warton. This was not how his wife was supposed to discover the truth. There were supposed to be lovemaking and breakfast and confessions.

"Perhaps we can take this to my study," Ambrose ground out.

"To hell with your study, I want to know where the hell you are keeping Holly!"

Ambrose folded his arms over his chest. "And what business do you have with her?"

"I know you took her against her will, which is kidnapping and against the bloody law."

"I did no—"

"You found my sister and did not think to inform me?" Willow accused, a mere whisper.

Ambrose blanched at the hurt in his wife's voice. He wanted to soothe her, take her into his arms, but with Warton standing on, looking smug as a cat, his limbs froze in place. Dammit, alone, after he tossed Warton out on his ass, he'd tell Willow the truth.

This was a family matter. And Warton was not family.

"It is of no concern—"

"Of mine? Holly is my sister. Am I to understand, then, that your brother is no concern of yours?"

Christ. That was not what he meant to say. Ambrose turned to his wife, his eyes imploring her to understand. "That is not what I said. Willow, let us talk—"

"As of yet, my father has not permitted the union. So you have no right to take her without her consent."

Ambrose stared into her despondent eyes. This was spiraling. He needed to get the matter straight with her now but doing it in front of Warton was out of the question. The man was intent on taking his anger out on him and was bound to twist anything Ambrose revealed.

"Your father agreed to consider my terms—one of which is that she may remain on my property until he has done so."

"He only agreed to your insanely idiotic terms because I am here to keep an eye on her. Where is my sister?"

"She's not here."

"You said—"

"I said on my property, not necessarily this property." How he hated Warton in this moment.

"You manipulative bastard."

No, wait.

Ambrose's heart lurched to his throat. When Warton whistled, emotion, wild and dangerous, whirled inside him, so he let the curtain drop over his features. He shot the man a look that promised swift retaliation.

Ambrose was mightily aware he was failing. He wanted to drop on a knee for his wife, explain, but first he must deal with Warton, the damn bastard. Then he'd grovel. "This is not the time, Willow."

"I beg to differ, this is the perfect time." She descended two more steps, the smell of her scent taunting him. "You are keeping my sister from me, and that is unforgivable. I thought we had discovered something magical between us, but it seems I was wrong. Know this: I may share a house with you, attend balls at your side, dine at the same table, but you are no longer my home, and you are no longer welcome in my life beyond that."

His heart plummeted to his feet like the hundred-year-old vase they'd knocked of its pillar at the Gallery.

No.

"You are my wife."

"She is my sister."

Their gazes held, one pleading and the other angry and hurt. Ambrose wanted to explain. The words were on the tip of his tongue, Warton be damned. But logic fled the moment he saw frost replace the fire in her eyes. He saw it there, the cold hard truth, reflected in her depths—she would not believe anything he proclaimed. She would only deem it as an excuse. She didn't trust him enough to believe him.

Anger overrode any and all sensibility then. Anger for not telling her earlier, anger for saying the wrong words now, but mostly anger directed at Warton, who had barged into his home, ruined his plan, and sparked his temper to such a degree that Ambrose was now digging a grave for his marriage.

How the hell did he come back from this?

He glanced at Warton with an arched brow. *Happy now, you bastard?* Out loud, he said, "Get the hell out of my house."

"This is preposterous, Ambrose. You cannot keep my sister from me, and you certainly cannot force her to marry your brother! Where is she?"

Dammit! He *had* to convince her he planned on doing the right thing. But if his original plan was gone, could he come up with another one to convince his wife of his sincerity? But how?

Unless…

A crazed idea sparked in his mind.

His eyes met hers. "On the contrary, my dear wife, I intend to do exactly that."

Pain flashed across her face, and he dug his fingers into the palm of his hands.

"What of your brother?" she asked, lifting her chin. "Does he not have a say in the matter?"

"Everyone seems overly concerned with my brother."

"There is no reasoning with you—not when you are this stubborn, this uncaring of who you hurt."

"Quite right, my dear." The shovel dug deeper—only this time, it was intentional.

Ambrose had no idea if his new plan would work, but it was the only one he could think of. Sensing Willow's withdrawal drove him a little mad. It rightly terrified him.

But he knew that if he simply said that Holly was free to go now, she'd never believe that he'd planned to do so in the morning in any case, that'd he'd made that choice of his own will rather than by force at a midnight confrontation.

And if she thought it by force, she'd never trust him. She would always be suspicious of him—doubtful of him. So, he'd have to convince her it was his choice another way—a ludicrous, nearly impossible way. He'd have to give up all control and let her do what she did best: meddle.

"Then know this: if you do not let this grievance go, you will never be welcome in my chambers again."

Ambrose braced himself, concealing the impact of that statement. He had a secondary plan and he was now depending on it to work. And for it to work, he needed to play the part of the beast.

"St. Ives," Warton barked. "As much as I am loath to interrupt your marital setback, I must warn you: if you harm one hair on Holly's head, I will disembowel you. As for your brother, I will disembowel him, too, if he agrees to your cockamamy scheme and marries her. In fact, I might eviscerate you both just for the sheer pleasure of it."

It was not difficult to be a beast for Warton.

"What is my sister-in-law to you? She has been nothing but a thorn in my side."

"I gave her my word," Warton said.

"Your word," Ambrose murmured. The man might be madder than Ambrose himself. "And you will incur my wrath over the word you gave a woman who left me, a duke, at his wedding?"

His wife made a gurgling sound in the back of her throat.

Fine, he knew he was an arrogant bastard. But he wasn't in a charitable mood. His wife was nearly lost to him and it was all Warton's damn fault. He knew that it would be a miserable path ahead to redemption and that he placed squarely on Warton's head. It was easier than feeling the keen regret of not telling Willow about Holly hours ago—the moment he'd made the decision to let Holly go.

"I am no more afraid of you than I am of a rat," Warton growled. "To me, her importance has never been in doubt. And let us not forget, you asked her to marry you under false pretenses."

"A mistake."

"You've made many of those, I see." Ambrose stiffened when Warton's gaze flicked to Willow. Bastard. "Hand her over, St. Ives. I will not ask again. I don't give a damn about you or your supposed wrath. It is paltry against what you will experience if you incur mine."

"I am the Duke of St. Ives, Warton. Do not forget it."

"A duke. A bastard. It's all the same to me. You speak as though you are untouchable, but are you? A man whose pride is so easily wounded that he keeps young women locked away as retribution? I tell you this: you might have Miss Middleton now, and you might even believe that you will marry her off to your brother, but that marriage will happen over my rotting carcass. You take my word for it."

Well, it was apparent that Warton loved the chit. It did not soften Ambrose's current fury towards him, however.

Ah yes, what was the beast's next line?

"She humiliated my family name."

"I don't give a damn. You already have one Middleton to make miserable for the rest of her life. I'll be damned if you take another."

Warton shot him one last glare before he turned and marched from the residence.

"I am not an enemy you want, Warton," Ambrose called out.

"Neither am I, St. Ives," Warton barked over his shoulder.

Ambrose watched Warton's retreating back, his breathing harsh.

"I can't believe you're holding my sister hostage while sharing my bed."

Ambrose turned to face his wife, but she was already ascending the stairs at a brisk pace, away from him.

For the first time in more years than he cared to admit, Ambrose had found something special, too special to let go. Willow made him feel things he'd never thought he'd ever come to feel. And he wasn't about to lose that.

He'd damn well slit his throat before he let that happen.

Unfortunately, what he needed to do was nearly as difficult.

Chapter 23

Impudent devil! Black hearted oaf! Conniving bastard! How dare he kiss her so warmly and tenderly with those deceptive lips of his! How dare he make her feel loved, all the while harboring her sister in secret. This went far beyond betrayal! It went . . . It went . . . Well, just too far!

Willow exploded into her chamber in high dudgeon, quickly turning to slam the door and lock into place. She jumped when a hand halted her fireworks, shoving the door open and filling the entrance.

"Get out," Willow snapped. Tears threatened to spill.

"We need to address this, Willow."

"I don't ever want to speak to you again!" she exclaimed, snatching a pillow and throwing it at him. "I mean nothing to you!"

"That's not true," he denied. "You are much more than nothing."

Willow gave a hollow laugh. "I thought to give you the benefit of doubt. I believed that this marriage could become more than what it started out as, but I was wrong. There is no heart in you."

"That's not true," he growled.

"The truth lies in your actions, Ambrose, and they seem clear to me."

"Damnation!" He ran a hand through his hair, a muscle working in his jaw. For a moment, it looked like her husband was going to say something—something crucial. But then he only looked away, a mask falling over his face.

"Nothing to say?" she mocked. "Of course not, once again you have disappeared behind your mask of control."

He remained silent.

Willow squared her shoulders. "What you did is reprehensible, and I cannot help but resent you for it, Ambrose."

"Willow, I—"

"No, do not lie to me. Your actions tell me all I need to know."

A pained look crossed his face before a look of determination replaced it. Silence settled between them.

Willow turned and paced across the chamber, stopping beside the fireplace, her heart in her throat. He was impossible to look at, stealing her ability to think, her ability to reason, to draw breath. She stared at the cold hearth, no embers crackling tonight. Her heart was breaking. For their future that suddenly seemed doomed. For her sister.

If there was no future for them, then perhaps they could at least finally have the truth.

"Why do you have a set of rules?" she asked, afraid to look at him, afraid he'd deny her this. He didn't.

"Eleven years ago, my sister fell ill." He paused, inhaled a ragged breath. "Celia never quite recovered from her illness, always getting tired early and sleeping late. She refused to allow those limitations to stilt her life. She lived to the fullest, or at least, as full as a thirteen-year-old girl could live—insisting on dance lessons, running barefoot in the country fields, and climbing trees—even when the physicians argued against it. She never once slowed down, until a year later, the strain on her heart was too much, and it just stopped beating. At least, that is what the doctor said."

She turned towards him. "I'm sorry . . ."

He raked a hand over his face. "He claimed her heart finally failed due to fast, unhealthy living. That we could have prevented an early death if we had kept her under lock and key."

Willow's heart slammed against her chest, and for a moment she couldn't breathe. She imagined him ten years ago, his ravaged features as he sat beside his sister's bed, blaming himself for not taking better care of her.

"It wasn't your fault," she whispered, clenching her fists into her skirts to keep herself from going to him.

"I could have prolonged her life if I had forced her to live a slow-paced, routine-filled life."

"She was sick, Ambrose, and your sister knew that. She chose to live her life on her terms. Had you forced her to live any other way, she'd have been miserable and passed on that way, too."

"But she could have lived longer if she'd lived by rules. Perhaps become well again." His obsidian eyes were shadowed with pain as they lifted to meet hers.

"That is no way to live." She motioned between them and the chamber. "We both deserve the freedom of our choices. Or else what is the point of living?"

"I agree."

"You agree?" Willow asked, taken aback.

"I know you are not my sister, Willow," he dragged a hand through his hair. "I will always believe I could have done more to save her, and I will always be a devil to live with, but that is why I have not enforced the rules with you. I didn't want you to feel like a prisoner in our home."

"Then why draw them up?"

He shook his head. "I only created them because when the reality set in that I was about to take a wife—become the protector of another woman—I panicked.

The pain of losing my sister rushed back, and I did not wish to go through that again."

His soft admission brought tears to her eyes. She blinked them away. Their gazes collided, and what she saw in them sent a burning sensation through her belly. She had fallen hopelessly in love with her husband.

"Now you know."

Yes, but it didn't change anything. It didn't change what he'd hidden from her or that he'd chosen grievance of her sister over their future.

Staring down at the doom of her future, Willow wondered at the next step. Liberate her sister, she supposed. After that was anyone's guess.

His eyes were guarded, watching her from beneath long lashes. He looked miserable, and Willow wanted to give in and fly to his arms. But she wouldn't.

"There was always the possibility you'd not change your mind," she closed her eyes before opening them again, "but I'd at least thought you'd inform me that you found my sister. That you planned on going through with your intentions."

The statement hung between them, silence stretching.

Curses! The man had her vacillating between wanting to kiss him and kill him. Willow glanced away from him, back to the empty fireside. To think only an hour ago they'd been happy. An hour ago, they had been sleeping in each other's arms, content and sated. An hour ago, she'd been thrilled by the prospect of a true family with Ambrose. Now . . . now she didn't know what she wanted.

She didn't know if she could ever forgive him.

She didn't know what that meant for her dreams.

"Please go."

"Willow..."

"Please, I just want to be alone," she practically begged. "I understand now, the way you are, but it doesn't change what happened. It does not change that you chose to keep my sister from me. It does tell me that I don't mean as much to you as I had begun to believe." She paused, keeping her eyes on the dead hearth almost symbolic in its appearance. "Please go."

Willow would plead no favors. She would not beg he release her sister. It was time to take matters into her own hands.

"Please just read the rules on your desk."

There was a moment of punishing silence, and only once the soft thud of his footsteps receded did Willow whirl around and glare at the door separating them. Honestly! He wanted her to read his rules at a time like this? After what he'd just confessed. Fine, she would read his blasted rules, *then* she would burn them, *then* she would go forth and purposefully break each and every one of them!

She marched over to the desk and tried to set them on fire with her eyes. When that failed, she snatched them up, fully intending to read them out loud—to scream them out at the adjoining room.

Boundaries for the Duchess of St. Ives.

What a lark. She flipped the page over to cry out the first rule at the top of her voice. Frowned. And flipped through the rest of the papers, examining them top to bottom, back to front.

They were all blank.

Much to her mortification, she burst into tears.

Ambrose strode back to his room, seething and despairing.

He should never have waited. He should have told her the moment his men informed him that they'd found Holly. But instead, he'd teetered with indecision and then pettily thought that Miss Middleton could wait a night for him to make his grand announcement.

Damn Warton to the seven bowls of hell. Everything had gone to shit and all because that bastard had marched into their home with thunder and bluster in the middle of the night. He'd trampled on Ambrose's plan and he'd ruined the ground Ambrose had gained with his wife.

With a curse, he paced the length of his chamber, dragging his hands through his hair. She had made no demands for him to release her sister, hadn't made the slightest reference to the fact, only stared into the empty hearth with a resignation he had put there. That alone confirmed what he'd realized standing on the stairs bickering with Warton.

Ambrose could no longer let Holly go. At least, not in the straight-forward manner.

His wife firmly believed he did not trust her, that all they had shared was a lie. He would never convince her he cared for her if he freed her sister from consequence now. She'd believe it an act, a tactic of some sort. She'd never believe him if he said he'd come to the decision before Warton ousted his secret. She'd never believe he was going to tell her in the morning. So, even if he released Holly, they'd never be able to overcome the matter. Willow had lost all trust in him.

Ambrose inhaled a deep breath.

And that is where the new, albeit highly difficult plan came into action. He'd known standing on those stairs, shaken and furious, that the only way forward was to give his wife space to be who she was at heart—a lovely, meddlesome creature. It was the only way Ambrose could see to make her understand he accepted her wholly, unreservedly, and without question. He passively allowed her to meddle. He'd give up control.

So she would devise a plan to free her sister.

And he would let her.

Once Holly was free, he'd make sure his wife understood that he'd sat back and surrendered long before she'd won.

His inaction would be his action.

He would give up the reins—like he had done with his new set of rules—and then, only then, would Willow believe that he was sincere. He damned well hoped. Prayed.

He sank down onto the bed, resting his head in his hands.

What a bloody disaster.

But it would be worth it. Because he loved her.

It was a truth he could no longer deny. Nor wanted to.

He loved his wife.

Chapter 24

"This is ridiculous, Jonathan. It will never work."

"It was *your* plan."

"Yes, but you ought to have pointed out how horribly it would fail." Her eyes flicked around her husband's study, reminding Willow of one little obstacle—her husband's intelligence. He was bound to see straight through their plan. Fortunately, he had given her space. *Verbal* space. Unfortunately, his presence—always lingering—touched her to the bone. It was there in each beating pulse under her skin, in the gooseflesh rippling over her arms. Her awareness of him was absolute.

As were those blank pages he had left on her desk.

They had called into question *everything*.

"It won't fail as long as he drinks the brandy."

"That's all well and good. But I have to drink the brandy, too, or at least give the appearance of drinking."

"As long as you don't drink more than a tiny sip, you'll be fine."

"And if he notices I'm not drinking?"

"Why would he notice that? You're a woman."

Willow turned to glare at him.

Jonathan held up his hands in surrender. "Just use words like freedom, separation, and *lover*. He will drink. Trust me."

Willow shook her head, unconvinced. "If I throw words like that around—mind you, I still don't know how I'm going to incorporate them into a sentence—Ambrose will most assuredly want to keep his wits about him and not drink."

"Trust me, little sister, there is no one alive who can navigate my brother's mind better than I—he will drink."

She scoffed, her eyes darting to the brandy in question. "How do you know?"

"Call it male intuition, but faced with the prospect of losing you, his wife, Ambrose will claw up to the ceiling."

Willow scrunched her brows together. "What?"

"His faculties will desert him," Jonathan clarified.

"That's assuming he had any in the first place."

"I believe he cares more about you than even he is aware."

Here's to hoping, Willow thought bitterly, then sighed.

Naturally, she felt she was partly to blame for her current predicament. In the course of her weeks married to Ambrose, she had ample time to fight for her sister. Instead, she had taken a subtler approach, attempting to work on the man rather than the matter. It mattered little that Willow had thought she'd have more time to persuade him to let his grievance go, or that she'd given him the benefit of the doubt to do the right thing. She'd still ended up here, having to orchestrate a kidnapping of her husband in service of her sister's future.

A future Jonathan had aided in securing when he discovered Holly's whereabouts and freed her. Whereupon her sister had made one request: A wedding.

Tomorrow.

Which brought them to this moment—attempting a hairbrained scheme to get Ambrose well and truly out of the way. Plus, the timeline gave them precious little time to not only remove him from the equation but also put together a wedding.

"I still cannot believe my sister fell in love again so soon. And with the Marquis of Warton, of all men! And after I told her not to!"

"The heart wants what the heart wants," Jonathan murmured. He cast her A Look. "Regardless of what you demand of it."

Willow stuck out her tongue. But her mind was already wandering back to those blank pages. She had thought Ambrose incapable of change after that fateful night she discovered his deception. Her mind *had* demanded she cut him loose. Her heart was stubbornly refusing.

To her heart, those pages resembled hope.

"Tell me the plan again."

Willow inhaled a fortifying breath. "Drive Ambrose to drink with silly words. Once he is passed out from whatever you laced it with, you will haul him up to my bedroom and bind him."

"You've given orders to the servants to remain clear of your chambers?"

Willow nodded.

"Marvelous."

"What if he doesn't believe I'm sincere?" So many things could go wrong. She could lose her nerve, for one.

"Trust me."

Willow gave Jonathan one last skeptical look before deciding to trust him. After all, no one knew Ambrose better than his brother. But she felt horrid for what she was about to do.

And then he was there, appearing in the doorway, handsome as sin and sculpted in stone. His gaze flicked between her and Jonathan before they narrowed.

"Am I interrupting?"

Willow smoothed her hands over her skirts. "No, I was—"

"Speak with your wife, Ambrose," Jonathan interrupted with a distinct note of disapproval. "And do recall our last conversation."

Willow flung her eyes to him. Every single line of Jonathan's face etched in stony disapproval. Remarkable! This was not a side of him she had ever seen or imagined existed. He was such a happy fellow.

Ambrose bore his eyes down on her, and she swallowed.

"Er, yes, well, I would like to speak with you."

Her husband arched a brow, entering. Jonathan gave a curt nod and strode from the room, not bothering to spare her so much as a parting good luck glance.

She squirmed, Ambrose's hard eyes penetrating deep into her soul. *You're doing this for Holly*, Willow reminded herself. *Just think about her*.

When she just hovered there, awkwardly intertwining her fingers, his brows furrowed.

"You wish to speak with me?"

Willow flushed at the mocking notes infused in his voice. It gave her the courage to hold her head high. "I wish to address the matter of our marriage."

Her palms were sweaty. Perspiration beat at her brow. If she were the swooning type, she'd be sprawled on the floor already.

"What about it?" He leaned casually against his desk, his arms crossing over his chest.

Lord, the man could be so infuriatingly composed at times. Anger sparked low in her belly.

"I want a separation."

He stared at her—unblinking—for a torturous moment before he stalked over to the decanter and poured two glasses of brandy. Jonathan had been right. Willow just hoped Ambrose swallowed his in one breath. Then, perhaps, she might not have to go any further with this charade. She was a terrible actress.

For a moment he said nothing, handing her a glass and taking a healthy swallow of his own, his gaze brooding.

Willow bit the inside of her lip to keep from blurting out something inappropriate. She took a small sip, merely touching the liquid to the tip of her tongue, really, and sank down in one of the armchairs. He mimicked her, settling in an opposite chair.

Heavens! She hoped he did not mimic her drinking progress or their plan was doomed.

"This arrangement—" she began.

"Marriage," he snapped, swallowing the entire glass and then jumping up to refill it. This time, he remained standing, so Willow stood as well, turning to him.

She studied his features. He had hardly shaved since their wedding day, the growth of hair staining his cheeks giving him a rugged appearance—not that of a polished duke.

Furthermore, he hadn't pushed her to read his rules, hadn't taken her over his knee for sneaking out at midnight. He hadn't even called out Warton for his insults.

All signs pointed to the possibility that perhaps he hadn't been *entirely* in control since their marriage.

But, here, in this moment, all signs of control were gone altogether. Oddly, the idea warmed her. Just as those blank pages had. Did they mean he was letting his rules go? They no longer existed? She wanted desperately to ask him about them but pushed the thought away. That was not part of the plan.

"Right," she said when he just continued to stare at her. "Marriage. I wish to be separated from it."

"Why?"

Why? Well . . . how was she to answer that?

"I . . . er . . ." What had Jonathan said? Something, something, and lover. "I wish to explore my options."

"Explore your options? What the hell does that mean?" He straightened to his full height.

Right. What did that mean?

"It means I do not feel valued." That sounded like something a woman leaving her husband might say.

"Valued? Christ." He took another swallow and then another, as if dealing with her line of reasoning was too much. Those coal black eyes delved deep into hers.

"Did you not feel valued when I had my hands all over your body, making love to you?"

Burning color instantly swept up her neck. "That is hardly the point."

"What is the point then? You can hardly claim to feel undervalued after you've come undone in my arms." His eyes narrowed on her. "Again and again."

Her entire body went weak. She bit down on her lower lip. "That is not the only way to measure feeling valued. Feeling respected is another. Trust is yet another. And I can't trust you anymore." Her voice was as trembly as her limbs, but she'd gotten through the sentence.

"Because I did not tell you I found your sister? I haven't harmed her. I haven't bloody married her off. And yet, you wish to leave me without so much as allowing for an explanation."

"You have given me all the reasons I need." *And all the reasons not to.*

"And for that, you'd toss me aside like a rag doll?"

"Perhaps you ought to have thought about that before you hid my sister from me."

He shut his eyes, pinching the bridge of his nose.

"There is more to marriage than finding pleasure with bed sport," Willow carried on, blissfully ignorant of the sudden tension in the room. "Why, a *lover* could give the same outcome, I'm certain."

His eyes snapped open, and instant fury clouded their depth. "There will be no lovers."

"Perhaps not now but one day, when our marriage has reached its inevitable moment of unfolding—"

"Stop."

Her mouth snapped shut at that single word, spoken with such menace that Willow grimaced. She watched as he took another swig of brandy.

"You drive me bloody insane," he muttered, his eyes glaring at her in accusation. "And you're too bloody beautiful for your own good."

"Only you would say something at a moment like this," Willow said, taken aback by his declaration.

One of his arms dangled at his side, the other barely holding up the glass, his movements sluggish. The draught was taking effect, Willow realized with relief. She wasn't sure how much more of this she could have endured.

"It must be working then," she murmured to herself.

"What's working? Not our cursed marriage, apparently."

"You're swearing a lot." She tentatively stepped towards him, hovering near him, just in case.

"I'll swear as much I damn well want to." His words slurred. What had Jonathan laced with the brandy?

"You're quite beautiful," he purred, leaning forward to cup her cheek in his hand.

"You already said that."

"I have?" He looked startled at the thought. "There is something else I need to confess."

"Yes?" Willow urged when he fell silent.

He stared into her eyes, drawing his brows together. "It slips my mind."

"You cannot recall anything?"

He thought about that, and then muttered. "Meant to let her go."

"Ambrose?" Willow shot forward when he began to slump, keeping him upward. "Meant to let who go?"

"Planned an entire feast."

"What are you talking about?" Willow asked. She had a hard time following his train of thought. He meant to let someone go and planned a feast? But before she could form a thought on his ramblings, his head slumped against her shoulder.

"Jonathan!" she cried.

"You like my brother better than me."

"That's not true."

"You do."

"I truly do not."

"Warton ruined everything, bastard. Was going to tell you, you know, and now you prefer my brother. Much better than me."

Dark eyes lifted to meet hers, stark longing reflected there. Her heart tugged, and Willow could not prevent the next words from tumbling out—no matter if she knew better, no matter if they might be already doomed.

"I prefer you," she whispered and dragged in a shaky breath. His shoulders leaned heavily into hers and Willow realized he was no longer aware of the world around him, so she said, "I will always prefer you, because despite everything, I think I might be in love with you."

At which her husband promptly crumbled to the ground.

"Jonathan!" Willow called out again, sinking down beside him.

Moments later, her brother-in-law strode into the room, his gaze flicking over them as he kneeled beside Ambrose. "Well, that didn't take long."

Not long? It felt as though it had taken everything from her. "He's going to be a beast when he regains consciousness."

"Better get him up to the room. I'm not sure how long he'll be asleep."

Her anxious eyes sprung to his. "I thought you said it would work!"

"And it has, though I cannot speak to how long the draught will keep him under, which is why we are tying him up."

Willow traced a finger over Ambrose's brow. This confrontation must have been the hardest thing she'd ever done, but she wanted to give Holly the best chance at a happy future. And if marriage to Warton made her sister happy, then Willow was happy.

But what did that mean for her? What had her husband attempted to confess? Had he planned on letting her sister go? What was this feast? When had he replaced his rules with a blank set? But more importantly, had she gotten it all wrong?

Softly spoken words lulled Ambrose back to awareness. Dreamish words. Pretty words. Words spoken from the lips of his wife.

I think I might be in love with you.

Lifting an arm to wipe at his lids, it snapped against resistance. He tugged again. What the devil? His eyes shot open to glare at his arm, which was bound to something—he angled his head up—the bedpost. He tugged at his leg, already suspecting that limb, too, would find resistance.

He was bloody tied down onto a bed.

Like a bloody sexual sacrifice.

His gaze snapped down to his body. Christ's sake, he wasn't even naked. Where was the joy in that?

His eyes swept the chamber, landing on his wife, who sat patiently waiting for him to . . . what? Wake up? How long had she been sitting there? Or rather, how long had he been tied up? His burning limbs told him too bloody long.

"What is the meaning of this?" he snapped. Or at least he tried to. His words came out a jumbled moan.

Disbelief tore through him.

His wife had not only tied him to the bed but shoved a stocking in his mouth! And wrapped it tightly around his head. The jumbled events in his brain suddenly snapped together. Jonathan. Willow. This must be part of their plan.

As if to taunt him, his brother appeared in the doorway, a happy smile on his face.

"Good evening, brother."

Was it evening already? *Well then, good evening, you little bastard.*

"Ambrose," his wife murmured, and his gaze ventured to her. She swallowed. "We have taken these measures for your own good."

Oh, really.

"We found Holly," she said, rising from the chair.

I gathered as much.

"And she is getting married to Warton tomorrow morning."

Ah, Warton. The son of a bitch isn't wasting his time.

"We will release you once the ceremony has concluded."

Oh, honey, I will be released much sooner than that.

His brother shifted against the frame, crossing his arms over his chest. "Best wait until the marriage has been consummated," Jonathan said, his grin wolfish. "Just to be sure."

Ambrose gave an inward snort. No man made an ass of himself like Warton had over a woman he hadn't already bedded *and* fallen in love with. He would have done the same, perhaps worse.

He ought to know. Just look at where love had recently landed him. Bound and gagged on a bed.

His wife nodded, drawing his attention away from his thoughts. "I suspect neither of them will leave anything up to chance." Blue sapphires sent him an apologetic glance. "I know you must be mad at me—"

No, love.

"For conspiring against you—"

I expected that—you did not disappoint.

"But I hope you will forgive us."

No forgiveness called for, love. Well, maybe he'd make Jonathan ask for some.

"What happens when we release him?" Jonathan chirped from the door.

"I'm not sure I follow?" Willow murmured with a brief glance at Jonathan.

"He will be furious," Jonathan said. "Do we release his bonds and let him stalk the chamber for two days before we let him out?"

Ambrose rolled his eyes.

"I will release him after the ceremony," Willow said, tucking a curl behind her ear. "I shall also be spending tonight with my sisters to prepare for the wedding."

Instant protest welled up. She was leaving? The sudden piercing memory of her earlier words in his study raided his mind, cascading down on him like a ton of bricks. And courtesy of his current predicament, Ambrose was in no position to voice his opinion or do something about it, so he let his displeasure flash in his eyes.

"I am not leaving, leaving, Ambrose." She cast an uncertain glance to Jonathan. "I said those things to goad you into drinking the brandy. But we do need to discuss some unresolved matters."

Oh, he had plenty to discuss.

He watched them take their leave, his hammering heart settling into a steady rhythm. That had been part of their plan, too? He was going to throttle his brother when this was over. As it were, Benson was going to have a fete when he discovered Ambrose—Ambrose was damn well never going to live it down.

Chapter 25

"I cannot believe I'm the last unmarried Middleton heathen," Poppy declared, snatching a lemon cake off a tray from a passing footman.

"We are not heathens," Willow corrected, contemplating the stairwell with interest. "We are just prone to trouble."

Poppy followed her gaze. "What do you think they are doing up there?"

"Talking," Willow murmured, a slight blush staining her cheeks.

"Talking? That's what Holly said." Poppy cut her a skeptical look. "Is that why we are blocking the stairwell?"

"We are ensuring their privacy so that they can discuss whatever matters they are . . . discussing."

"Yes, yes, if kisses were words . . . they have been talking a long time."

Well over an hour, to be exact.

Warton had carried her sister up the stairs after a passionate kiss over an hour ago and they had yet to reappear. And they were not talking. Of that Willow was certain.

It had been a blast catching up with her sisters. Like old times. They discovered that three of the duke's lackeys had captured Holly and brought her back. Fortunately, Holly had been treated well, except for a minor incident with a horse, or Willow would have been tempted to leave Ambrose tied up indefinitely.

Speaking of her husband, while staying at Belle's had been wonderful, Willow missed her home . . . and her surly husband.

Again and again, those blasted sheets of white paper filled her mind. His half-muttered confession. What was she to make of it all? Had it truly sounded as if he was trying to tell her he had planned to let her sister go all along or was that just her imagination wishing for it to be the case? Was there more to the story than she was aware? Her mind was a puddle of confusion.

And as if the situation wasn't complicated enough, she definitely loved the blasted man.

A twinge of guilt pinched her heart at leaving him tied up and locked in a room for the entire night—until she reminded herself that he deserved every bit of that time to think about his actions.

"I'm sure they will be down shortly," Willow said, snapping out of her thoughts.

"Perhaps I shall meet my future husband today," Poppy murmured. "Would that not be splendid?"

"There are no guests at the wedding, only family," Willow pointed out.

"There is the delectable Mr. Marcus Hunt," Poppy pointed out with a wistful smile. "Bow Street Runner extraordinaire."

"And he is much too smart to fall for your tricks."

Poppy laughed. "You may be right," she said. Thunder rolled in the distance. "At least we saved the cake. Do you think Holly will mind a wedding in the drawing room?"

"I doubt the bride or groom will notice," Willow mused.

The front door was suddenly flung open, and a man stepped through. He was tall, soaked to the bone, and handsome as sin. Leaves rustled in alongside his boots as he stepped over the threshold, his eyes instantly landing on her.

Willow stared at Ambrose in outright amazement. Drops of rain coated his hair and face. He wore no cravat, and his shirt gaped open at his chest. He looked wild. Predatory.

The tiny hairs on her nape leaped to life.

"Is that not your husband?" Poppy asked. "I thought you said you tied him up."

She did. *They* did. But no words formed on her tongue.

"Is this going to turn into one of those disasters you only read about in the papers?" Poppy whispered from the corner of her mouth.

Maybe. Probably. Lord, Willow prayed not.

Her pulse leaped in her throat. There was a sudden sting in her breast and she felt heat gather at her core. His gaze cut right through her until she feared her knees might give out. His eyes were focused and unblinking, locked onto her as he walked over to them.

"Willow."

She inhaled sharply. Her breath froze in her lungs. His voice was pitched so low it found its way beneath her skin, sliding into her bloodstream.

Gooseflesh spread all over her body.

"How did you . . ." Her lips parted and shut again. "Where did you . . . I . . ."

"Is there a question in there, love?"

To her astonishment, amusement colored his voice. Was he laughing at her? Had he just called her "love"? After they had drugged him and tied him up? She cast Poppy a perplexing look, who, in return, lifted her shoulders in a careless shrug.

"You're too late, St. Ives," Poppy piped up when Willow failed to speak. "My sister and Warton are reunited, and I daresay wild horses could not drag those two away from each other."

"I see. Am I too late for cake then, too?"

"Excuse me?" Willow croaked, at last finding her voice. "Cake?"

A smile tugged at his lips. "I'm quite famished, having been tied down to my bed for an entire night. The experience has made me fancy a slice of cake." His eyes swept over the rushing servants. "Wedding cake, I presume?"

Willow blinked up at her husband. Ambrose, her stoic imperious duke, was casually talking about cake as if he *hadn't* been tied up for an entire night. Was this a trick? He sounded so *amendable*.

"Is there some place we can talk?" he suddenly asked. "Or do you wish to hash this out before an audience?"

Willow cast a brief glance at Poppy who looked much too intrigued for her liking. "No, let's go . . ." Her eyes swept the hall for a spot of privacy.

"Home?" Ambrose suggested. "I, for one, would not mind settling this in the privacy of our bed."

Poppy made a gurgling sound.

Color swept up Willow's neck to her cheeks. "What? You . . . That . . . *No*." Willow glanced around uncertainly.

"Then shall we stay and enjoy the wedding with your family first?"

Willow's head jerked back to him, reading only sincerity in his obsidian eyes. "You want to stay for the wedding?"

He shrugged. "Why not?"

"I'm missing something here, aren't I?" Poppy said.

Willow paid her sister no mind. "Why are you behaving like this?" she asked, her eyes darting to Lord Jonathan, who had suddenly entered the hall from the drawing room.

"Like what?"

Willow met her husband's gaze and motioned at his person. "Amused. Happy. Humorous. Not like yourself."

"I am more myself at this moment than I've been in the last ten years, love."

"And why are you calling me 'love'?" she asked with a skeptical scowl. "I tied you up and you aren't even angry?"

"And he's smiling," Poppy remarked. "It's making my skin crawl. Downright scary."

"I only wish to talk," Ambrose insisted. "I mean no trouble."

"And about what do you wish to talk?" Willow challenged.

"My feelings. Apparently, believe it or not, I have a ton of those," Ambrose said, his eyes never leaving hers.

"You do?" Willow blurted. She hadn't meant to sound so surprised, but merciful heavens, he'd said the word *feelings*.

"Of course, I believe it's the nature of humans to have those."

"You're human?" Poppy muttered.

Willow shook her head. "I meant . . . What I meant is that you have them—feelings—for me?"

"Of course. Is that not clear by now? I will say that I never expected you to drug me and tie me up, though I should have, I suppose. You hail from the Middleton bloodline, after all."

"You . . . you . . ." Willow spluttered, staring at him wide-eyed.

"Orchestrated this," Poppy finished in awe. "He orchestrated it all."

"I did no such thing," Ambrose denied.

"But you let us free my sister, knowing some sort of rescue would be underway." Willow's brows narrowed speculatively. "Why?"

"Madness, mostly, but I suppose that's to be expected when one falls in love with one's wife and has to find a way to prove it to her."

Jonathan's laughter crackled through the air. "Well, I'll be damned."

Willow sucked in a breath, her eyes glued to his. The lines of his face were cut deep, but the hard edge to his features was gone. Lord, had he just told her he *loved* her? The brandy and sleeping draught must still be in effect. That's it. He couldn't possibly have said that.

"Then why did you not call off your henchman?" Willow demanded.

"I was too late."

"And when you learned they found Holly? Why not let her go then?"

"I planned on releasing her, but Warton ruined the surprise."

"*Surprise*?"

Ambrose nodded. "I planned on letting her go that very morning. You were supposed to enter the dining room, feast spread out, your sister smiling at the table."

Willow swore she felt her heart melt there and then. "Why did you not tell me then?"

He took a step forward. "I froze, love, and behaved like an ass. I truly never meant for it to go this far."

"You still could have told me," Willow said in a small whisper, her heart pumping madly.

"Would you have believed my sincerity? That I had decided to let go of any grievance before my men found her? Before Warton barged in and yelled bloody murder?"

"I . . ." Would she have? Perhaps not. No, definitely not. She'd never have believed him, not in that moment—for why hold Holly without telling her if he decided not to go through with his plan?

As if sensing her thoughts, he added, "It all happened so fast, much faster than I expected, and before I knew it, I had your sister tucked away and no damn clue what to do with her. Then Warton ruined my plan. It was supposed to be romantic."

"So you sat back and did nothing?" Poppy asked, looking more fascinated by their conversation than she ought to.

Honestly.

Ambrose nodded. "I knew, for me to convince Willow of my sincerity, I had to give up the reins and let her do what she does best. Which, in this case, would mean rallying the troops and liberating your sister."

"Which happened," Willow murmured, inhaling the earthy scent of her husband—he smelled of tobacco and rain. She allowed it to fill her senses, to wash away the doubt that clenched around her bones. But first, she had to make sure . . . "So you were not planning on forcing a match between my sister and your brother?"

He shook his head, staring at her with those dark, intense eyes. "I've recently come to appreciate the word *more*."

More.

She knew the feeling tied to that word well.

Willow felt a smile spreading across her face. "You shall have to tell me about this word and how you have come to appreciate it."

The corners of his mouth lifted. "I am looking forward to doing just that."

"Wait a minute," Poppy interrupted their spell. "Can we please revisit the part where a husband falls in love with his wife and all that?"

"Oh!" Willow exclaimed. "I'd like to revisit that too."

"Was I not clear enough?" Ambrose asked. A grin broke out on his face.

"Not nearly clear enough," Willow proclaimed.

"Then I shall be clearer," he murmured and dropped his head to take her mouth in an achingly sweet kiss. A kiss that conveyed much more than words.

He lifted his head slowly, his eyes burning into hers. "I love you."

Willow sighed, content. "I might have gathered as much."

He arched a brow. "You did?"

"Your set of rules, I read them. But honestly, Ambrose," Willow teased. "I haven't a clue how to read blank pages."

"I'll help you. They read: My heart belongs to you, and always will."

Suddenly, it was hard to breathe. It felt like her heart would simply explode right there on the stairs. Sweet Mary. Her husband *truly* loved her. He had given up his rules *for her*.

How was she supposed to respond to that? This was no small thing. Of course she loved him back. And now that he'd told her the truth of what happened with Holly, now that he'd given up his rules, there was nothing to hold her back from flying into his arms.

"Do you love me, Willow?" he asked when she only stared at him, at a loss for words.

"Of course she does!" Poppy exclaimed with exaggeration. "It's the most obvious thing in the world."

"Botheration, Poppy! Must you be so forward!" Willow chastised, though she nevertheless found herself grinning up at Ambrose. "But she might be right."

"What the hell is going on here?" Dashwood thundered, filing into the hall, along with the rest of her family.

Another botheration!

A low growl deep in Ambrose's chest was the only warning she received before she was swung up in her husband's arms, him ascending the stairs two at a time.

"Where the hell is the bride and groom?" Dashwood snapped behind them. "And where are those two rushing off to in such a hurry?"

"Take the third room to the left," Poppy called out after them, her laughter following them up the stairs.

Epilogue

"Shouldn't we go down? Everyone must be wondering what happened to us," Willow murmured.

Ambrose twisted a golden lock of his wife's hair around his finger, kissing the tip of her nose. He loved her so much it damned hurt his heart. The emotion flooded him, wholly consumed every part of him.

"Everyone knows what we are up to," he drawled, rolling onto his back so that she sprawled over his chest.

"They cannot possibly suspect!"

"That your husband ravaged you after confessing his undying love, hauling your pretty behind up the stairs, and disappearing for hours?"

"It hardly happened that way."

"I recall it happening exactly that way."

"Except for the confession of *undying* love part."

His hands moved over her back, cupping her buttocks. He whispered into her ear, "Did I not use the word undying?"

She shook her head. "You mentioned something about falling in love, and affections, that is all."

He rolled her over so that she was beneath him, his mouth crashing down on hers in a deep, stirring kiss before he said, "I told you there is no place where you could go that I could not find you, but the truth is there is no place where you could go that I would not follow. I'm at your mercy Willow, and I love you, un-bloody-dyingly."

She giggled. "That's not a word." There was a short pause. "But I'd rather stay right here in your arms than go anywhere on earth without you."

Emotion clogged his throat. "Are you going to answer my damn question or not?"

"And what question would that be?"

"The one where you tell me that you love me back, that I am the most irresistible man on earth, and that you cannot possibly live without me."

"Oh, *that* question." She traced a finger over his lips, and he shuddered. "I do."

"You do *what*?"

"Find you irresistible." Her lashes fluttered provocatively.

"Willow," he growled.

"Oh, fine!" She stretched her mouth into a half-smile. "I cannot possibly live without you—I've grown quite fond of Cook."

"Damnation, woman! Do you love me or not?"

Laughter poured from her lips. "I confess, I confess! I do. I love you, quite madly, in fact."

The breath left his body. "You make me the bloody happiest man ever."

Her hands skimmed over his chest, lowering until her fingers curled around his throbbing erection. "I can make you even happier." She squeezed.

Ambrose dropped his head to her neck in a low groan, his lips already trailing kisses along the slope of her breast. "If we keep this up, we might as well take up residence."

"And fill my cousin's hall with babies."

He rose up to lightly drop a soft kiss on her lips before grinning down at her. "Fair-haired little creatures with sky blue eyes."

She blinked, stunned that he'd imagined their family, that he was of same mind as she. At last, his mask had fallen away and in his eyes Willow found nothing but love. Joy swelled inside her. All of her dreams were coming true.

"I'm rather partial to dark eyes." There was an odd tremble in her voice.

"Are you now?" he murmured and brushed his lips across hers. This time, he didn't come up for air, not for a very long while.

They entered the drawing room a while later, just in time to witness the bride and groom exchanging vows, surrounded by their families who stood in a half circle along the edges of the room. It was far from a grand setting of a church but it was much more romantic. The couple stood before the hearth, eyes locked onto one another, the glow of the fire illuminating them in soft light. Clothing rumpled and hair tousled beyond repair, the couple made quite a sight.

It was the perfect Middleton wedding.

"You two look no better than them," Poppy leaned close to whisper into Willow's ear.

Willow hid a smile, sparing a glance at her thoroughly disheveled husband. He looked rather wild. Untamed.

She loved it.

As if he sensed her regard, he glanced down at her, fire flashing in his gaze. "Woman, you have thoroughly corrupted me."

"Well," Willow murmured teasingly, "it was about time someone took it upon themselves to do so."

"I am in your debt," he murmured in reply. Then, after a moment, in a low, hoarse voice, he added, "We should go in search of the wedding cake. I can think of a few things we can do with the icing."

"For Christ's sake, have some mercy," Poppy groaned from her other side. "Unmarried lone woman over here."

Willow stifled a laugh. "You are not a lone woman."

"I certainly feel like one listening to you two *and* watching those two practically devouring each other with their eyes."

"Jonathan is eligible, you know," Willow said with a mischievous smile. "You might consider him—"

"Do not start, I beg of you. I prefer men with impossibly arrogant swaggers, if you recall."

Willow chuckled just as the ceremony ended with Warton sweeping his new bride into a passionate kiss, eliciting another groan from Poppy. No sooner had the family congratulated the couple then Holly rushed over to them, Warton in tow.

Willow cast a nervous glance to her husband. "Please behave," she murmured sweetly through her smile.

Warton's dark countenance, on the other hand, did not bode well, nor did Ambrose's cool stare.

Holly cast an uncertain glance at Ambrose.

"Ambrose," Willow warned.

He sighed. Heavily. "I believe felicitations are in order," he said to no one in particular.

Willow cleared her throat. Honestly, men could be so high handed at times.

"And please accept my apology," he continued begrudgingly.

Warton's brow shot up.

"Lord, they are like dogs sniffing each other," Poppy muttered. "And to think I was envious."

This time Holly jabbed an elbow into her husband's ribs.

"Bloody hell, fine!" Warton glowered at Ambrose. He nearly choked on the word. "Accepted."

Holly clapped her hands together and beamed at the two men. "Smashing!" She turned to Willow, eyeing the duke's arm around her waist. "We have some catching up to do, it seems."

Warton made a protesting sound.

Ambrose growled low in his throat.

It appeared there was only so much the men would tolerate.

Willow blushed under her sister's curious scrutiny, but not before her husband swooped her into his arms and carried her from the room. "You can catch up later, Lady Warton," he said over his shoulder. "At the moment, we have babies to make."

About the Author

Tanya Wilde developed a passion for reading when she had nothing better to do than lurk in the library during her lunch breaks. Her love affair with pen and paper followed soon after she had devoured all of the library's historical romance books!

When she's not meddling in the lives of her characters or drinking copious amounts of coffee, she's off on adventures with her partner in crime.

Wilde lives in a town at the foot of the Outeniqua Mountains, South Africa.

Made in the USA
Monee, IL
30 July 2025